P9-BAT-710
AR B.L.: 4.2
Points: 3.0

BANDIT'S MOON

SID FLEISCHMAN

BANDIT'S MOON

ILLUSTRATIONS BY
JOS. A. SMITH

GREENWILLOW BOOKS NEW YORK

www.williammorrow.com
Printed in the United States of America
First Edition
10 9 8 7 6 5 4 3

Library of Congress Cataloging-in-Publication Data

Fleischman, Sid, (date)
Bandit's moon / by Sid Fleischman,
illustrations by Joseph A. Smith.
p. cm.
Summary: Twelve-year-old Annyrose relates her adventures
with Joaquín Murieta and his band of outlaws in the
California gold-mining region during the mid-1800s.
ISBN 0-688-15830-7
1. Murieta, Joaquín, d. 1853—Juvenile fiction.
[1. Murieta, Joaquín, d. 1853—Fiction.
2. Robbers and outlaws—Fiction.
3. California—Gold discoveries—Fiction.]
I. Smith, Joseph A. (Joseph Anthony), ill. II. Title.
PZ7.F5992Ban 1998
[Fic]—dc21
97-36197 CIP AC

Especially for
Susan Hirschman

CONTENTS

CHAPTER 1

I HIDE

I had hardly got three miles down the road when O. O. Mary herself caught me running away and locked me up in the harness room off the barn. It was infernally dark, and I knew there were black widow spiders in there. I tried to keep my mind off them except to think that O. O. Mary could give black widows lessons in meanness.

I had been padlocked almost a week when I heard someone come around the pond on a winded horse, frightening off the squawking ducks and mud hens. I heard a yell: "Mary! O. O. Mary! That Mexican's a-coming after you! The whole gang of 'em! Run for your life! They ain't far behind!"

It was hardly a moment before a key started rattling

in the padlock. O. O. Mary flung open the door. The white afternoon sunlight about blinded me.

She tore through the saddles and harnesses and general trash until she came up with a scuffed red hatbox with the tips of yellow feathers sticking out the lid. I'd been using the box to eat on when she remembered to bring me some food.

I could hardly imagine that she'd ever owned a pretty hat. She had a head of hair as matted as a dead cat's. But hadn't I heard her say she'd once been with the circus or a showboat or something? That must have been a hundred years ago, I thought. I don't know what her real name was. She told me that everyone called her O. O. because her eyes were always open, and don't forget it.

She gave the leather box a smile with that fossil face of hers and then seemed to notice me for the first time.

"Out of my way, child! Run for your life!"

"What on earth for?"

"Annyrose! Didn't you hear? That cutthroat don't spare women and children! Why are you standing there? Contrary orphan! Run!"

"I'm not exactly an orphan," I said. After all, I had kin. I had a brother still alive.

"It's no skin off my bones if that confounded outlaw murders you in your shoes!"

If I'd wanted to argue fine points with her, I'd have reminded her they weren't my shoes, either. She'd sold my New Orleans petticoats and dresses months ago. She had me walking around in some boy's cast-offs, shirt and pants, and brown boots as curled up as dead fish.

"Don't claim I didn't warn you!" she shouted, pushing me out of the way. "And don't think he'll spare you! It's the devil on horseback riding this way! It's Wakeen himself!"

I answered, calm and snooty, "He isn't coming after me."

"Stupid girl!" she snapped. "His arms drip blood up to his elbows. And if he don't finish you, there's Three-Fingered Jack to do it. They'll cackle over your bones, the whole gang of them! Pesky foreigners! Greasers!"

That was what she called her Mexican help, when she had any. The foul and lumpish woman didn't have a good word for anyone. "You don't aim on coming back, do you?" I asked, hoping I might be seeing the last of her forever.

"Even if they burn the place to the ground, I'll be back," she snapped.

Moments later I saw her with her hatbox racing down the road in her dusty black buggy. It was piled with loose dresses and her big goose-feather mattress, all rolled up and puffy as a cloud. With the horsewhip held aloft, she struck sparks in the air.

I'd heard the horrible tales about Wakeen, and they *were* enough to give anyone the fits. Now, as I saw dust rising behind the hill, I decided I ought not to be passing the time on the porch having myself a long fresh drink out of the water barrel.

I got my few belongings in a pillow slip, in case the outlaws set the ranch on fire. My eyes lit on the bundles of hay standing out in the field like a flock of scarecrows. With my bootheels flopping in the dirt, I hurried to the field and snugged myself inside the nearest stack of hay—but not too deep. I wanted to be able to see the famous cutthroat.

As I waited, I thought I must be a true child of calamity to be standing all covered with smelly hay. Ever since we'd set out for California, my mother and brother, Lank, and I, bad luck came leaping out at us. Crossing Panama on muleback to reach our ship in the Pacific Ocean, Mama had caught a jungle fever. We had had to bury her at sea off the coast of Mexico.

When Lank and I landed in San Diego, where Mama

had planned to start a school, our money was stolen right out of Lank's left coat pocket. Not only our money but all our papers, including a guide to the gold country up north that Lank had got hold of. It showed an *X* mark near a place called Mariposa where there was supposed to be a rich vein of gold.

In order to eat, we had had to sell off Mama's trunkful of books, including all of Shakespeare in red leather bindings. And then Lank got it into his head to walk to the gold diggings a few hundred miles north, the both of us, and strike it rich like everybody else. He figured we'd outfit ourselves in Sacramento first. So we set out with all our belongings on our backs like peddlers. But you'd think someone had thrown a curse over me.

Mama never believed in evil curses and hokeypokey stuff like that, so I figured bad luck just happened. And when it did, Mama never spared it more than ten minutes of her time and just got on with things. I tried to get on with things, but why couldn't I have tripped over my own long feet and broken my ankle in a better spot? Lank carried me to the nearest house, which was only a mile away. Tarnation! It turned out to be O. O. Mary's horse ranch.

Only she was just back from across the border in

Mexico, and so powdered and gussied up you'd hardly recognize her. She splinted my leg with greasewood sticks and seemed as kindly as your grandmother. So Lank left me there to heal and said he'd send coach fare as soon as he could. And she said not to worry, for as soon as I could walk on my leg, I could do little things around the horse ranch to earn my keep.

Lank was hardly out of sight when she pulled off her wig and put it in mothballs. The next day I found her holding up my dresses and lace petticoats to the light. They disappeared to pay for my keep. I cried when she sold my violin in its black leather case and every note of my Mozart and Schubert. She even cut off my long yellow hair and sold it.

With all the comings and goings around the place, it didn't take me long to figure out that she dealt in stolen horses and earrings and anything else you didn't hang on to with both hands and a foot. I think she must have stolen letters from Lank. He wrote me once from Sacramento to say he'd be sending me coach fare, but I never saw it.

I was awakened from my thoughts by the squawk of ducks from the pond. When I looked out again, there came the bandits, about ten of them, with their hawk's eyes looking out from the black shade of large straw hats. Yellow cartridge belts made *X* marks across their chests. The men looked as stiff as soldiers, and I wondered if they'd fought in the war we'd finished off with Mexico. The Mexicans had sold us California and Texas when it was over, but when it was over, my papa didn't come back. Closer and closer the horsemen came, walking their beasts now, with only the silver jingle of spurs and the snort of a horse to disturb the afternoon quiet.

I recognized a big Mexican by the finger missing off his right hand and figured he must be Three-Fingered Jack. My gaze shifted to the bandit riding beside him, the one with the silver buttons running down his legs. He smiled. His teeth gave off a flash as white as oyster shells. That must be Wakeen, I thought.

He made my blood run cold, smiles or not. I'd never been so near to murdering villains. It surprised me that Wakeen hardly appeared much older than my brother, Lank, who was seventeen. And the outlaw wasn't even as tall. He wore a red scarf around his long black hair so that he looked more like a pirate than a general leading his army of cutthroats. Step by step he advanced. He frightened me even though his arms weren't stained with blood all the way up to his elbows.

He smoked a thin black cigar as crooked as a twig and wore silver spurs almost as big and spiky as sunflowers. He said something in Spanish, and his men began ransacking the place, looking for O. O. Mary. He dismounted and helped himself to the water dipper on the porch.

As I peered out, I saw him staring down at the dust, studying it. He must have had a keen eye for tracking because he began following my fresh footsteps as directly as if I'd left a trail of breadcrumbs like the kids in the fairy tale. I saw him pull a pistol from his sash, shift to one side, and cock back the trigger.

"*Buenas tardes,* Calico. I heard a whisper that O. O. Mary was hiding you. Do you wish a moment to say your last prayers? It is me, Wakeen!"

I was almost afraid to breathe. If the outlaw saw even a few straws jiggle, he might be edgy enough to fire.

"Did you think I wouldn't hunt you down, eh, you and your unpleasant friends? *Sí,* one by one. Did you hear about your *compadre,* Mountain Jake, who carried off my dear Carmela? I used him to start a new cemetery on the road to Angels Camp. And your friend Smiley, who helped you hang my dear young brother—poor Smiley, he smiles no more. And now

I have caught up with you, *Señor* Billy Calico. Shall I allow you three seconds to beg for mercy, the same time you gave my brother?"

"Don't pull that cursed trigger!" I burst out, feeling that the occasion called for strong language. "I'm not Calico!"

"Eh?"

My heart was banging away. "I'm not even full grown! I'm just a child, sir!"

"What? In such big shoes?"

"They're not mine."

He paused. "You have a gun?"

"Of course not!"

"No?"

"See for yourself."

Striking through the straw, his hand caught me by the neck like a chicken and pulled me out into the sunlight. I fluttered my fingers in the air to show that my hands weren't hiding anything.

"So it's only a skinny boy," he remarked.

"I'm not a—"

I cut myself off. Of course he thought I was a boy in these clodhopper boots and pants. As a sudden notion burst into my head, I decided not to correct him.

"I'll give you another chance, *muchacho*," he said.

"Run for your life! I am the terrible Wakeen!" And he crossed his eyes and showed his teeth in a snarl.

I stood there, just studying him over and waiting for him to stop showing off.

Finally he put the cigar back into his mouth. "You are not frightened?" he asked. "Don't you believe the stories about me?"

"Some of them," I said. "But no man could be that heartless and cruel."

"But the *gringos* are."

"What are *gringos*?"

"You," he said. "You Yankees who try to drive us Mexicans off this land."

"I'm not a Yankee," I said. "I'm from Vermilion Parish, Louisiana."

"You are all Yankees. You steal our gold and shoot at us for target practice. So perhaps I should shoot you just as a matter of obligation to my people."

"Well, I'd be obliged if you didn't," I said.

Three-Fingered Jack rode over, a big, round man with so many knives sticking out of his belt that he looked like a porcupine. "*Ay,* again Calico has escaped us. But look, there are fresh buggy tracks, no?"

"We follow them,"

"You'll be wasting your time," I said, even though

no one was asking my opinion on anything. "That was only O. O. Mary flying out of here."

Wakeen bent his knees and almost sat on his spurs. "There was a man with her?" he asked, peering into my eyes. "A thick-necked man with wild red hair? Hair like a bonfire!"

"No, sir. There hasn't been anyone staying here but me. Not for months that I know of."

"You are sure?"

"Positive."

He gave a faint sigh and puffed smelly smoke out of his cigar. "Then my spies are mistaken. Three-Fingered, tell the men to mount up. We might as well go home. We head north."

"I burn the place down, yes?"

"And leave our calling card to see for miles around? You forget, *amigo,* we are hunted men."

I'd been in California long enough to know that *amigo* was Mexican talk for "friend."

Three-Fingered Jack said, "And the horses?"

"Pick out only the best animals, *bandido.* Wakeen does not steal trash."

Moments later the outlaws were milling about, driving horses out of the barn and helping themselves to saddles. Wakeen watched for a moment and then mounted his own horse, a frisky black stallion with a tail that swept almost to the ground. I hitched up my suspenders and followed him, carrying my pillowcase full of belongings with me. In my haste a couple of things fell out. He pulled on the round leather hat that had been hanging by a thong from his neck. "*Adiós*, Yankee," he said, giving me a little salute with his fingertips. "I will shoot you another time."

"Mr. Wakeen—"

"Give my regards to the chief of police, eh?"

"Sir! Don't turn me back to O. O. Mary. Take me with you!"

He paused. He reined his horse into a tight circle and looked down at me again. "You are *loco*? Crazy?"

"I won't go back to O. O. Mary," I said defiantly. The thought of running off with Mexicans, who'd been my father's enemies, made me uneasy. But my mind was made up. O. O. Mary would be too afraid of him to chase after me. "Let me go with you!"

"I cannot have a noisy infant to look after."

"I'm not an infant—I'm almost twelve. And I'm not noisy. Please, sir! You won't have to look after me. If I can get to Sacramento, I'll find my brother."

"*Adiós!*"

"I won't be in your way! I promise!"

"Go back to your schoolbooks, *muchacho.*"

With a gloved hand he pointed to the book that had fallen out of the pillowcase. It wasn't a schoolbook. It was my mother's recipe book, which I'd kept.

"Please! Please! Let me ride out of here with you, sir!"

I didn't notice that Wakeen had posted a lookout until I heard a sudden racket from the hilltop. A horseman came racing down through the clumps of green cactus, shouting his lungs out.

"Wakeen! A posse! Twelve, fourteen men! Riding this way!"

"What took them so long?" said Wakeen with a brief smile. Then he looked off toward the sunset sky, his eyes tightening. "Don't the *gringos* know they can't capture a desperate outlaw like Wakeen at this time of day? I will have to teach them a lesson."

Biting his cigar, he spurred his horse and vanished inside the dust cloud rising about his men and horses.

I gazed after him, wanting to break into tears, but suddenly I was too angry to cry. He might not want a girl along to get in the way, but I'd let him think I was a boy. Wakeen had plenty of horses. He could have let me ride along with him. He was a cold-hearted varmint after all.

Suddenly he reappeared. He had spun his horse around and now was riding back toward me. He seized up on the reins.

"That book, *muchacho.* You can read it?" he asked.

"Of course," I said.

"Every word?"

"Most of them."

"Pick it up," he said.

I gathered up the book. He reached down to me, and I grabbed his arm like a life preserver. I could feel the great strength in his arm as he hoisted me behind him on the horse.

"*Sí,* I will let you ride with us, Yankee," he said.

I was dumbfounded. "You aim to learn how to bake biscuits, sir?"

"Don't ask stupid questions."

"But it's a cookbook!"

He gave a small, indifferent shrug. "Will it tell me how to cook the *gringo*'s goose, eh? Hang on, *muchacho.*"

CHAPTER 2

THE BUCKSKIN HORSE

We left a cloud of dust behind us that I supposed could be spotted clear from China. But I didn't see Wakeen once glance behind him. I guess he figured if no one was shooting at him, he was far enough ahead.

We were riding into the night end of the sky. We rounded some boulders and dropped into a riverbed. It hardly had enough water in it to splash, but our dust vanished.

Still, I could see our tracks in the wet sand and felt on edge. A blind mole could follow us. When bullets began to fly, I knew I'd be as much a target as anybody in the band. But when I thought that at last I was free of O. O. Mary, I could hardly hold back my smiles.

We followed the riverbed until well after dark, when Wakeen finally stopped to loosen the saddles and rest the horses. That's when he checked the livestock and picked out a horse and walked it over to me. It was a long-haired buckskin that pranced around as if she weren't entirely broke.

"You will need a fast horse to keep up. You like this one?"

"She's beautiful," I said. He called one of his men for a saddle and began cinching up the leather.

"I give it to you. A gift from Wakeen the Terrible."

I shot him a look. It was easy to give away something that wasn't his. "I'll ride it, but I won't keep it. It's stolen."

"Ay, Dios mío!" he exclaimed, letting out an exasperated sigh between his teeth. "Who puts such unkind thoughts in your head?"

"That's what you do, isn't it? Steal horses?"

"*Muchacho,* you see Pio Pio over there trying to swim like a sardine in one inch of river water? In Santa Barbara he found a rope on the ground. When he dragged the rope to camp, we found a horse on the other end. Is not finders keepers among Yankees?"

"Stolen," I muttered. "I can't keep it."

"Holy as a priest, this *gringo*!" he exclaimed. "Suit

yourself. But name her. How can a horse have any self-respect if she has no name, *bandido*?"

I looked back at him, startled. If I was traveling with bandits, did that make me a *bandido,* too?

Wakeen gave a signal, and the men mounted their horses. I climbed into the saddle and kept a length or two behind Wakeen and Three-Fingered Jack. Riding in darkness, we continued in the riverbed.

The buckskin could have been a little less snorty and intimidating, and I had to keep my reins up tight. I had the feeling that if I gave her the slightest chance, the mare would try to throw me. She just seemed to be waiting to let me know who was in charge.

I wasn't sure now that Wakeen had done me a wonderful favor in choosing the light-skinned buckskin for me to ride. I began to notice that my horse showed up ghostlike in the dark. I saw that the other outlaws rode dark animals, and Wakeen's was so black it turned invisible at night. With the posse racing after us, I felt marked.

We kept to the river for half the night. The bed narrowed and deepened so that the horses were now splashing up water. When finally we stopped, I was a bundle of aches. Even the hair on my neck seemed to hurt.

"Sir," I said, "if it would amuse you to get me killed, say so straight out. With the posse after us, you know I'm marked on that buckskin."

"I know no such thing." Then he laughed with contempt. "The posse! That handful of thumbs! They're making camp."

"How can you be sure?" I asked.

"If they want to catch Wakeen, tell them, Yankee, not to let the sun go down. How can they catch me in the night, eh? Under a bandit's moon?"

"I don't see a scrap of moon," I said.

"*Sí.* That is why it is a bandit's moon. The *gringos* cannot follow horse tracks they cannot see. They are making camp. You will be safe on the buckskin."

A moment later I saw how cleverly the wheels spun in his outlaw head. He saw a way to use the horses he'd stolen from O. O. Mary.

Together with Three-Fingered Jack and Pio Pio, he slapped the flanks of the horses and started yelling, "Go home! Run! Make your own trail for the Yankees! Go! Go home!"

The outlaws waved their hats until they'd run the small herd off across the scrubby flats. In the morning the posse would find clear tracks cutting west.

Wakeen gave a signal to mount up again. The

thought of climbing into that creaking saddle once more was as unpleasant to me as it must have been to the buckskin. But I did it. We continued following the river until the sun rose like a blinding white light. We made camp in the shade of a runty willow tree. I stretched out in the dirt and fell asleep.

CHAPTER 3

EATING CACTUS

A foot kicked me awake. "Get something to eat. Soon everything will be picked."

It was Pio Pio, the outlaw who'd found a piece of rope and discovered the buckskin attached. When my eyes cleared, I took a hard look at him. I don't think he was fourteen years old.

"You didn't have to kick me," I said.

"You're a *gringo,* no?" He gave me a flickering smile, as if he meant to insult me in the nicest possible way. His face was round with his black hair as stiff as wire. "Wakeen said to show you how to eat."

"I know how to eat," I answered.

"Follow me."

I ached. When I got up, I realized that during the

night's ride I had stored up enough pain to last me a week. Pio Pio led me toward his fellow outlaws, who were climbing like pack rats around a big rambling patch of cactus. "What are they doing?" I asked.

He didn't answer. He slipped in among the green leaves, but I stopped short. The leaves were as thick and flat as pancakes but covered all over with sharp spines. The plant looked as fanged as a nest of rattlesnakes.

Pio Pio drew his knife and cut off a bright red ball growing at the edge of a cactus leaf. He threw it my way. It rolled to a stop near my feet and lay there as prickly as a pincushion.

I gazed down at it. "Tarnation, you don't expect me to eat that?" I said.

That must have struck him as a dumb *gringo* question. I had a feeling that he wasn't entirely joyous at having to look after me. He kept tossing out more of the red pincushions. The outlaws were doing the same, laughing as if this were a treasure hunt—and yelping in pain when the cactus drew blood.

Like the other outlaws, Pio Pio used weeds to scrub off the hairy spines in the river and wash them away. Then I watched him slice off the top, peel down to something green and juicy inside, and eat.

"What is it?" I asked. I wasn't sure I was hungry enough to eat cactus.

"Las tunas," Pio Pio said. Didn't I know anything? He bit up a mouthful of the inside. "Cactus apples."

I decided I was hungry enough. "What does it taste like?"

"Like skunk. Do you have something better to eat?"

He quickly slit a cactus apple and handed it to me.

I discovered that I wasn't only hungry but starved. I wished I were back home, back in my mother's kitchen before we set out for the West. But I shook that picture out of my head before I teared up. Boys weren't supposed to shoot out tears, were they?

I picked up the defanged pincushion carefully and gave it a sniff. It smelled fresh. Pio Pio was kidding about the skunk. After a taste I went at my breakfast noisily and with enthusiasm, the way Pio Pio did. The cactus apple was shot through with small seeds, like grape seeds, and I spit them out all around. The pulp that remained was sweet. Pio Pio seemed pleased with the juicy sounds I was making and trimmed me another.

"How old are you?" I asked.

"Old enough," he said.

"How long have you been an outlaw?"

"I don't know. A year, maybe."

"How come? What happened?"

He turned his big dark eyes on me. "You *gringos* drove us off my father's *rancho.*"

"Me?" I protested. "I've never laid eyes on your *rancho*!"

"You *gringos* stole everything. The gold we were digging, our cattle, even a pot of chili out of the oven. Everything."

"Stop calling me a *gringo.* Those thieves were no friends of mine! Why didn't you go to the sheriff? There are laws, you know."

"*Sí,* Yankee laws. What good is that? The *gringos* chased us with clubs. We had to run for our lives."

"I don't believe it," I said.

"You don't know anything," he said simply.

"What did you do?"

"I run away and join Wakeen. The same as you."

Not the same as me, I thought. I was running away, but not to become an outlaw. "What about your family?" I asked.

His expression brightened. "Wakeen looks after them. At the hideout."

I don't think he saw my eyebrows rise. What hideout? But then I reminded myself that hideouts were none of my affair. All that concerned me was that I was now beyond the reach of O. O. Mary.

Not far off I saw Wakeen help gather dead wood for a bonfire now flaming up. I watched the smoke carried along on the morning breeze.

"Isn't Wakeen leaving his calling card?" I asked.

"What?"

"The smoke. Won't the posse spot it?"

Pio Pio gave out a smile, which on his round face seemed twice its actual size. "The great Wakeen no longer worries about the men of the posse. They will follow the stolen horses. *Sí,* like a dog chasing its own tail."

The outlaws were now swinging long knives, lopping off green cactus leaves the size of soup plates. These they began flinging into the fire.

I wanted to ask what they were doing, but I didn't want to keep asking dumb *gringo* questions. As if reading my mind, Pio Pio said, "To burn off the cactus needles."

"You outlaws eat the leaves?"

"To feed the horses. Don't you know anything?"

I watched the cactus needles catch fire, like so many little candles, and quickly burn out with twists of smoke. Pio Pio stationed himself at the fire, spearing leaves that were singed and ready for the animals.

He flung a blackened piece that landed with a few sparks at my feet. I supposed he meant it for the horse I'd been riding, so I picked it up. At that moment I caught Wakeen's eyes on me. I didn't want him to think that I couldn't take care of myself, so I approached the pale buckskin as if I knew exactly what I was doing. I held out the cactus leaf to the horse's lips. She ate it away in a couple of crunchy bites. I went back to the fire and got her a couple more pieces.

Wakeen came over and hunkered down, again almost sitting on his spurs.

"We sleep for a few hours. Then you start my lessons," he said.

I looked at him. "What lessons?"

"You will teach me your language."

"But you can already speak English."

"Can I read the signs on the roads, eh? Can I read what holdups the newspapers blame on me? Sadly, no. So you will teach me to read."

"But I've never taught anyone anything before."

"You will learn, *muchacho.* And I will learn, yes? For Wakeen needs to read about gold shipments and *gringo* posses looking for him, eh? And when he sees his picture on the sheriff's posters, he wants to know what they are offering for his head. Ignorance does not serve me well!"

I took a slow breath and let it out. I hadn't planned on hanging around with outlaws long enough to teach anyone to read.

CHAPTER 4

THE POSTER ON THE TREE

Once we mounted up, Wakeen had me ride beside him with my mother's cookbook open in my hands.

"Begin," he said.

"Here's a recipe for herring pie."

"What is herring?"

"It's a fish. See this. This is an *H*."

He leaned over and looked where I had my finger. "An *H*."

"Yes. And this is an *E*."

He took the book from me for a closer look. Then he said, "Is there a word here with a *J*?"

"Of course. 'Jelly' has a *J* in it."

"Show me."

I took back the book and found him a *J*. He studied the letter carefully.

"They tell me my name starts with a *J*. Yes, I have seen that shape on wanted posters. First, you must teach me to read and write my name."

"But your name doesn't have a *J* in it," I said. "Unless it's there in your last name."

"I am Wakeen Murieta."

"There's no *J* in your last name, either," I said.

"You are certain?"

"I'm positive."

"That's a puzzle, Yankee."

Flipping the pages back and forth, from the *w* in "crawfish" to the *k* in kitchen and the *n* in "lemon," I spelled out his first name.

He learned fast. Within a few days, as we wound our way north through the mountains, he could write his name in the dirt.

"How much farther is it to Sacramento?" I asked.

"A long way."

Even though my brother had headed there, it would surprise me to bump into him on the streets. The gold diggings were in the mountains somewhere, and that was where I expected Lank to be. I'd find him somehow.

Poking along, we returned to the herring pie, and he was soon reading off whole words. " 'Take white pickled herrings, and bill them—' "

"Boil them," I said, sounding, I thought, like a bona fide schoolteacher.

Three-Fingered Jack listened to all this with a sour face. He'd shift his great stomach and look us over with his bulging bullfrog eyes. Finally he pulled up even with Wakeen. "Why you letting this *gringo* ride with us? He will learn our secrets, no?"

"What secrets do we have, old friend? Is there a sheriff anywhere in California who doesn't know we are bandits?"

"But the *gringo* will know our plans."

"What plans?"

"You will think of one."

"My only plan is to stay alive, *bandido.* And to make life unpleasant for the Yankees."

I wished they'd stop talking about Yankees and *gringos* as if I didn't exist. It wasn't my fault they'd lost the war. I wasn't even sure what all the fighting was about.

Three-Fingered Jack gave me another bulging glance and then turned back to Wakeen. "Chief," he said, "the trouble with you is you trust everyone."

Wakeen gave out a soft laugh. "And the trouble with you is that you trust no one. Not even yourself."

I was beginning to feel distinctly uneasy. It was true, I *was* learning secrets. I knew they had a hideout. I wished Pio Pio hadn't let that slip. I wanted to know nothing. I felt suddenly fearful about what I had got myself into. If I learned too much, Wakeen would never let me go alive.

Wakeen turned to me. "My three-fingered friend worries like an old man," he said with a playful little laugh. "Do you know how he lost that finger, Yankee? I tell you. Biting his nail! *Sí.* By time he realized it, he had chewed the finger down to the knuckle. Is that not true, García?"

The big outlaw, whose real name I now learned was García, snorted and turned his horse and rode ahead. I had a feeling that he allowed only Wakeen to tease him.

As we approached the main road north, we began traveling almost entirely at night. "When the sheriffs and deputies are home, sound asleep!" Wakeen told me with a wink.

Days we remained hidden among the trees. It surprised me that no one saw through my disguise and realized that I was a girl. Maybe it was because I had got as dusty and dirty as everyone else.

It was just past dawn when we came upon a wanted poster nailed to the trunk of a gnarly oak tree crawling with red ants. Wakeen sat on his horse, with one leg crossed over the saddle horn, and tried to read the words.

"See how famous I am!" he said, aglow with pride.

The poster looked fresh. It showed a woodcut picture of a wild-eyed bandit with a flaring nose and a ragged black beard. It hardly looked like Wakeen at all, except for the scarf around his long hair.

"The picture is an insult," said Wakeen. "Am I not uglier than that?"

He laughed, and everyone laughed, for he had bold and handsome features.

Three-Fingered Jack came up closer and gave the poster a squint. "Maybe it's supposed to be me, no?" he said.

"You flatter yourself, *amigo*. Who would pay gold for the head of Three-Fingered Jack? Remind me to have a picture made of Wakeen himself for the sheriff. It would be a shame if they strung up the wrong man."

"*Sí*, send a picture with a flower between your teeth to charm the ladies," said Three-Fingered Jack.

"Why not?" said the outlaw. Then he shifted his attention to the words but was unable to find his name.

"Where is it, Yankee?" he asked, motioning me forward. "Where does it say Wakeen?"

$1000
EWARD
FOR THE
HEAD
OF
OAQUIN

"It doesn't," I said. "That poster says there's a reward for a bandit called Joaquín." I did my best to pronounce the strange name.

"But that's me!" He laughed. "*Sí,* didn't I tell you to put a *J* in my name? I knew there was a *J*!"

I stared at the poster again. Tarnation, was it possible that somehow I had taught him to spell his name wrong? As I gazed at the lettering, I wondered if the *J* might sound kind of windy in Spanish. Joaquín would then sound like Wakeen. That must be it! We'd have to start over again.

Joaquín tossed me a glance. "So what does it say, exactly, Yankee? There are too many big words."

I wiped the dust off my lips and read aloud, "One Thousand Dollar Reward for the Head of Joaquín, Dead or Alive."

"Ay, Dios mío!" exclaimed Three-Fingered Jack.

"So little!" exclaimed Joaquín with an air of insult. Then he said, "We will rest here."

Around the tree, with the wanted poster hanging like a parlor picture, the outlaws dismounted and made camp. After a breakfast of coffee and canned oysters, Joaquín fished a piece of charcoal out of the fire and let it cool. Finally he stood up and called for silence. With a show of bravado, he struck out the

$1,000 reward figure on the poster. Then he told me to hold his hand and guide the charcoal as he told me what to write.

When the job was finished, the poster read:

I WILL GIVE $10,000.
JOAQUÍN!

CHAPTER 5

"I AM JOAQUÍN!"

We must have been approaching the gold diggings, for an air of fresh adventure came over Joaquín. We rested at a Mexican *rancho* where Joaquín had friends. He seemed to pick up news that excited him.

The next morning he studied wagon tracks in the Mariposa road, as he called it, and smiled. The name caught my attention. Mariposa was the name on the map stolen out of my brother Lank's pocket.

Joaquín directed his men up onto the boulders and smiled. There the bandits waited, smiling to themselves and hardly talking. They sunned themselves like lizards for two days.

I was glad to stop, for I was burning with fever and felt wobbly in the saddle. I curled up in some dry leaves, and when I barked out a cough, Joaquín came running over.

"Be silent!" he commanded.

"I couldn't help it," I said.

He pulled off the red scarf from around his head. "Bite on this. If I hear coughing, I shoot you."

I could see from the fire in his eyes that he meant it. There was no doubt in my mind that he was planning a holdup even though he had allowed lone horsemen to ride by quietly. I wondered how scared the travelers would be to know they had passed under the eyes of the terrible bandit Joaquín.

I pulled myself deeper into the trees, as if to separate myself from the outlaws, and muffled a cough. I was glad to close my eyes, for I wanted to see nothing. But could I let innocent people coming along the road fall into a bandit ambush?

I wondered what my mother would do, but I didn't wonder long. I knew. She'd let out a cough to sound a warning and snap her fingers at Joaquín. I wondered if I had the courage.

I lay in a gloomy sweat, not sure what I would do until I heard a coach come thundering down the road. That was what Joaquín had been waiting for, I thought. That was why he had let smaller game ride by.

There could be women and children in that coach, I thought. I sat up and saw Three-Fingered Jack ready to leap off the boulder with a knife clamped between his teeth.

I yanked the red scarf out of my mouth and barked out a cough. But at that moment there was such a banging of pots and pans from the coach, and such a sudden blasting of guns, that I could no more be heard than a whisper in a storm.

But Joaquín heard. Later, after the bandits had relieved the coach of saddlebags of gold, he stood over me. "I warned you. Didn't you believe me?"

"Of course I did," I said. "I'm perishing of this fever, anyway. Go ahead and shoot."

He let out a six-cornered oath in his own language and carried me to the buckskin. After throwing me into the saddle, he used a lariat to tie me like a parcel to the saddle horn so I wouldn't fall off. The rope burned my arms and my waist. I began yelling that my fever was better already. But he wouldn't listen. Maybe he just meant to punish me. He gave a wave of his hand to his men, and off we went.

I was about dead when we made camp. He told Pio Pio to find a dried-out old acorn. Joaquín shelled it and, using a silver dollar as an anvil, pounded the nut into a powder. Pio Pio seemed to know what was coming, for he brought over a gourd of water. I suddenly realized that Joaquín intended to doctor me.

"Open your mouth."

"I feel better!" I exclaimed.

"Open!"

He poured the acorn powder down my throat. It tasted bitter as ashes. Pio Pio poured water down me, and they both stood back, as if to see me jump up, cured.

"It's the Indian way to smash a fever," said Joaquín.

"I'm cured," I said, forcing out a smile. That wasn't exactly true, but I did feel a little better and I didn't want a second dose. "How much farther to Sacramento?"

"Don't be a pest, Yankee."

A few nights later I heard Three-Fingered Jack say that we were so close to Hornitos that he could almost hear the fiddles at the dance hall. I wished I had a map so I could see where Hornitos stood. I knew that California was long and slightly bent and that the city of Sacramento and the mountain diggings were in the bend.

I might skip Sacramento, I thought, and head directly for the diggings, which must be getting close by. I might run into Lank, big as life, on one of these woodsy roads.

The foothills had grown steep, and we followed a narrow trail through a lot of brambles and smelly weeds—hogweeds, Pio Pio called them. The moon was hanging so bright I could see my own shadow. We might as well have been traveling in broad daylight.

We came out onto a level road, and I was bobbing about, half asleep in the saddle, when we stopped. I looked up and saw a nervous man with a reddish blanket thrown over one shoulder. He sat on a tall, rawboned horse with silver pistols in his hands.

"I am Joaquín!" he shouted. "Reach for the moon!"

"You are the famous bandit?" asked the real Joaquín with exaggerated awe. "The cunning one with a price on his head?"

"The same, *hombre*!"

"I didn't think he was so jumpy in the eyes and so long in the face. And where, *señor,* is your bloodthirsty friend Three-Fingered Jack?"

"Him? In the bushes with a rifle in each hand. Over there! *Sí,* all of my *bandidos* wait to pull their triggers. Throw down your gold, *hombre*!"

"Tell me, is it true that Three-Fingered Jack pulls the trigger with his thumb? Or does he pull it with his toes?"

"Deliver!"

"Of course, *señor.* But look at the fine red *serape*

over your shoulder. From Chile, that blanket, eh? And the spurs, too. Is the great Joaquín a *chileno*?"

"*Hombre,* do you wish to talk yourself to death?"

"But it is an honor to meet the brave and fearless Joaquín. Take our few measly bags of gold dust. This will be something to tell our grandchildren." He turned to his men. "*Muchachos!* Throw down our saddlebags."

I think the impostor was as surprised as I was to see the riches so generously thrown to his feet. The gold stolen from the coach was changing hands fast, I thought. Joaquín directed Pio Pio to load the saddlebags across the rump of the rawboned horse.

A moment later the impostor spurred his horse, and Joaquín gave him a playful salute of farewell. "Until we meet again, *chileno*."

I sensed there was a trick up his sleeve. An outlaw like Joaquín wouldn't give up heavy bags of gold without a fight.

"You see, Yankee," he said, grinning, as if to instruct me in the art of staying alive in the gold country, "I never argue with a nervous man holding pistols in his hands. They were shaking like Chilean earthquakes. He might have shot my horse."

Then he turned to a few of his men. "Claudio! Valenzuela! Pio Pio! Bring back the saddlebags. Throw your rope around the fool. Warn him to find a new line of work or Joaquín will not be so generous with his life the next time. These clumsy impostors will ruin my reputation."

The three bandits leaped forward in the moonlight. I wondered how Joaquín could be so confident that his men would catch the stranger. He sat on his horse, purring as contentedly as a cat.

"Tell me, Yankee, do you think I take too many chances, letting the *chileno* get away?" he asked, and I wondered why he cared what I thought. Maybe he needed to show off a bit before a *gringo* like me. "But that's my nature."

"The gold wasn't yours, anyway."

He said, "I'll tell you a thing about gold, Yankee. It makes an *hombre*'s head spin, eh? Out comes greed. It grows like mold! Didn't you see the mold in the *chileno*'s eyes when he allowed Pio Pio to burden his horse with one saddlebag after the other? He forgot that gold is heavy as lead. How can he win a horse race with an extra two hundred pounds of gold on his back, eh?"

Hardly twenty minutes passed before Claudio and Valenzuela and Pio Pio came trotting back with smiles and the saddlebags.

CHAPTER 6

I AM BLINDFOLDED

Joaquín hardly missed a day trying to read through my mother's cookbook. He had the alphabet down pat. We'd long ago finished with the herring pie, and we were under way on Dutch biscuits.

It was then that he had Pio Pio blindfold me, and that's the way I rode all night long through the smell of pine trees and the scolding of mockingbirds. It seemed no great mystery to me why he didn't want me to see where we were going. The bandits must be heading for their hideout. Why didn't he just turn me loose?

The blindfold was fine with me. I didn't want to know where the bandits hid out.

We passed into a narrow and windy passage through

the boulders. My horse seemed unhappy with the rocky, tumbledown footing and scraped me against one wall and then the other. My horse? I had to remind myself that the stolen buckskin belonged to someone else.

But she had got used to me clinging to her back. She no longer gave sudden kicks as if to warn me I might go flying through the air at any moment. I kept her brushed and washed her once from a pan and a trickle of mountain water. Outside of my brother, Lank, she was coming to seem like my closest friend. I'd even talked to her a couple of times, telling her why she couldn't have a name. "It'll be so much harder to give you up, horse, if I hang a name on you. Like you were family. So you're just 'horse.' Anyway, I intend to slip away from these bandits as soon as Joaquín can read a little better. I'm honor-bound to hold up my part of the bargain. He saved me from O. O. Mary, don't forget."

Suddenly I heard new voices and wild greetings. When Pio Pio snapped off the blindfold, I saw that we were in a small canyon with sheer brown cliffs. There were several cook fires scattered about the clearing, each fire throwing its own monster shadows against the night wall of the canyon.

Joaquín must have had thirty men waiting in the hideout—and a few women, too. There were corrals for horses while cows and pigs and sheep ran free. As if Joaquín had been expected, a whole hog was being roasted on a spit.

No one showed the slightest suspicion of me, as if people were accustomed to Joaquín's bringing in strays. Didn't they notice that this time he'd brought in a white-faced Yankee? Maybe it didn't show after weeks in the mountains and foothills. I supposed I had weathered like a shingle. I must be brown as a roast potato.

I saw Pio Pio slip off his horse and politely embrace a man with coarse white hair and a hanging mustache and then a woman with braided hair—his father and mother, for sure, I thought. And lucky him, I thought. Who would ever embrace me when I got home—if I could even figure where home was anymore?

I kept to the shadows, and before long a young woman in a whirling green skirt handed me a shallow wooden bowl. "Joaquín said not to look so unhappy. Eat!"

I wished he would stop keeping such a close eye on me. That would make it harder to slip away when the time came.

She gave me a playful shove toward the plank tables laid out for the feast. A couple of fiddles were already beginning to tune up. I yearned to pick one up, but I couldn't have played their tunes.

The woman gave her green skirt another whirl and danced a couple of steps, snapping her fingers in the air. I found out later that her name was Rosita and that she hoped to marry Joaquín. That didn't seem a good idea to me. He was bound to be caught, and she'd be visiting the cemetery a lot.

A couple of women were patting pancakes between their hands and frying them. Pio Pio moved up beside me. "*Tortillas,*" he explained, and used one to roll up beans and pork and a red sauce floating with seeds. I did the same. His mouth gloriously full, he watched me as if he expected to break out laughing at any moment. He hardly had to wait at all. The sauce turned out to be three-quarters prairie fire. I fanned my mouth and ran, gasping for water.

"You still have a *gringo* stomach," said Pio Pio.

Nevertheless, for the first time in weeks I filled myself right to the top and then lay back in the grass and gazed at the stars. It surprised me that I felt so content in this hidden canyon in the company of rogues and bandits, most of whom would hang. A guitar almost as big as a bathtub joined the fiddles, and Rosita began dancing in the dirt.

After a while Three-Fingered Jack himself joined her, dancing as quickly and lightly on his feet as a squirrel.

Pio Pio returned to sit beside me. I reckoned that Joaquín had told him to stick to me like flypaper. I had a strong feeling that he'd never known a *gringo* to talk to and regarded me as the next thing to a freak. Yet he was too polite to ask me questions, not even my name. These bandits were all that way, I'd noticed. Maybe it was a code among outlaws. Or maybe Mexicans were born polite. I'd decided to give out the name Zachary, but nobody asked.

We watched Three-Fingered Jack stomp his feet and laugh, and Pio Pio offered me some advice. "Don't cross him. Three-Fingered Jack is touchy as gunpowder."

"I'll be careful."

"Do you know how he lost his finger?"

"No."

"During the war on the Texas border," Pio Pio said, "some *gringo* shot it off."

I stiffened. My father had been there on the Texas border. What if he had shot off that finger? If the thought occurred to Three-Fingered Jack, he wouldn't hesitate. He'd strangle me on the spot.

But for all I knew, Three-Fingered Jack had fired the shot that brought down my father. The thought put me in a sudden lather of sweat. Then I gave my head a sharp shake, to stop my imagination from running away with me.

"What had they been fighting about, anyway?" Pio Pio asked.

"The war? I don't know for sure," I said. "I think both sides wanted Texas."

"But why? Weren't there enough cactus and rattlesnakes to go around? And now you got California, too. This earth between my fingers was once Mexico! I was born here, like my father and his father and his father, but the *gringos* call us foreigners. They are the foreigners, true?"

"True," I said.

"But Joaquín evens the score," said Pio Pio with a huge glow of a smile. "He is a great man, yes? You agree?"

"But he's an outlaw. He robs innocent people."

"He was innocent, too. He bothered nobody, digging his gold claim with his brother. Do you see any wanted posters for *Señor* Calico and his friends, who grabbed the diggings for themselves? Did you know they tied Joaquín to a tree to watch them hang his brother? Look. See Rosita dancing? Where is her sister Carmela that Joaquín had married? She has never again been seen alive. So, *gringo*, my father told me that Joaquín the Peaceful became the Terrible Joaquín—in the snap of a finger. No one will hang him. He is too clever!"

He was clever enough, as I'd seen for myself. But when I looked over at Joaquín, who'd now joined in the dancing, I kept seeing him with a scratchy sheriff's rope around his neck. I warned myself not to let his smiles melt me, the way they had Rosita and Pio Pio and everyone else. I mustn't forget that despite his acts of revenge, he was a rampaging cutthroat.

Later Three-Fingered Jack got possession of a large white quilt to sleep on and snored the night away under a pine tree.

First thing in the morning Joaquín awakened me. "Yankee!" he said. "Rosita doesn't believe I can read. Bring the book!"

I dug out the recipes and followed him to one of the morning cook fires. I handed him the book.

" 'Herring Pie,' " he read, in a voice as full as an actor's on the stage.

"What's herring?" asked Rosita.

"Some poisonous Yankee fish."

"It's not poisonous," I said. "But you do have to be awfully hungry."

Joaquín went on. " 'Take white pickled herrings, boil them a little . . .' "

He went on for a few more sentences, letter perfect except for the word *cinnamon.* Rosita's dark eyes went wide as Joaquín demonstrated his amazing feat.

"You must learn to read, too, Rosita," he said. "The Yankee *muchacho* will teach you."

Me? My heart gave an awful plunk. Did he think he was going to keep me here until I was full grown? He was now pointing to a tall woman with a child in her arm as she scattered grain for the chickens. "You see *Señora* Campos there. She would still be feeding chickens on her *rancho* if she could read. *Sì.* The law posted a notice that we had to pay land taxes, but who among us could read English? The miners smiled and waited for the deadline to pass. Then, like the pounce of a lizard's tongue on a fly, they swallowed her *rancho*. Do you want that to happen to you, Rosita?"

"I own nothing to tax," she said, laughing. "Perhaps only you, Joaquín. Is there a tax on you?"

"Of course. But for Joaquín they call it a reward."

Around the fires I'd heard enough tales of villainy

that I no longer doubted them. Gold miners had flooded in from all over the world with the high-and-mightiness of conquerors. They wrote laws to pry off those with darker skins from the diggings. But I wasn't willing to believe that all the *gringos* in California were tricksters and rogues. My mother wouldn't have been a party to such greedy goings-on. Not my brother, either. Most Yankees didn't go around stealing pennies off the eyes of a dead man. Only trash like O. O. Mary would do such things.

Where was the honor in mistreating others? I was sorry that Joaquín had declared war along the roads, for he was robbing innocent people, the same as the miners. Soon everyone would have a cause for bloody revenge. And where was the honor in calling each other prickly names?

I was lost in these thoughts when I realized that Pio Pio's white-haired father was standing before Joaquín.

"*Patrón,*" he was saying, "is there a mistake? It is certain the man Calico was hiding near San Diego. My cousin, a blacksmith like me, recognized him while shoeing his horse at O. O. Mary's."

"Your cousin was mistaken," said Joaquín simply.

"You looked everywhere?"

"Of course."

Suddenly I all but went weak in the knees. The

sight of Three-Fingered Jack rolling himself up in a white quilt the night before now sprang to mind. I remembered the sight of O. O. Mary with her wrapped-up quilt when she raced her buggy away from the ranch. I gulped. What if—

I wanted to keep my thought to myself. But I had assured Joaquín that the villain he was looking for hadn't been at O. O. Mary's. What if I had been wrong? My mother would have looked Joaquín squarely in the eye and said . . .

"Sir," said I, "I may have made a mistake about Mr. Calico. It just came to me."

"Later, Yankee," remarked Joaquín, still in quiet conversation with Pio Pio's father.

"But, sir," I said, "it's possible that the man *was* hiding at O. O. Mary's after all!"

"You would have seen him, Yankee. You said so yourself. Don't worry about it. There is plenty of time for revenge. I let him sweat awhile longer, eh?"

I spoke a little louder. "O. O. Mary had me locked up in a shed off the barn. For almost a week. He could have been in the ranch house, and I wouldn't have known it."

Joaquín now gave me a sharpening look. "Did you see him grow wings and fly away as we came up, eh?"

"Not exactly. But when O. O. Mary whipped her

buggy out of there, she had her big feather mattress with her. What if he was rolled up inside?"

He gazed at me for a long time, so long that my toes began to curl. Then he called to Three-Fingered Jack. "String up this Yankee," he said, and walked away. But he didn't say it loud enough for anyone to hear but me.

For a couple of days I seemed to have gone invisible. Joaquín looked through me as if I were so much window glass. But then he sent Pio Pio for me and the cookbook, and we resumed his lessons as if nothing had happened.

I was coming to feel that the book cast a spell that would keep me safe. He wasn't going to let anything happen to me until he learned to read. But he was learning so fast that we were soon turning the last pages of the book.

Suddenly I asked boldly, "Why do you bother? You will surely hang."

"Will I?" He gave a little smile and added, *"Es destino."*

"What does that mean?"

"It's destiny, eh?"

Es destino. I was to hear him say that a hundred times.

CHAPTER 7

THE CUNNING SCHEME

Joaquín kept me blindfolded while the gang wound its way out of the hideout. Somewhere in the foothills I could hear Three-Fingered Jack and the others turn off. It wouldn't surprise me if they'd be lying in ambush for Yankees and other prey along the roads. I wondered if there was a more dim-witted way to make a living. What would they do with their riches, hanging from the limb of a tree? I hoped Pio Pio wouldn't end up that way.

I was left, still blindfolded, riding alone beside Joaquín. He finally announced that we would be going into town.

My heart gave a little bounce. Was he going to turn me loose?

"But what if I yell for the sheriff?" I asked. "I could collect the reward."

I'm sure he had already considered that. He gave a snort and asked, "Is that how you would repay my hospitality, Yankee?"

"But you are an outlaw," I said.

"Only to the *gringos*. They offer a reward, but was I ever tried before a judge and declared guilty? No, *muchacho*. But the law has put a price on my head, anyway."

"But you do steal horses."

"And worse!"

I said, "I'm sure the law would be pleased to give you a trial."

"Sí," he answered merrily, and burst into a laugh. "But first, Yankee, your countrymen must catch me!"

He didn't take the blindfold off me until we camped, and for the first time I saw that he had changed his appearance. He was wearing a *gringo* suit, a starched collar and a black tie that hung at his throat like a dead bat. I guessed he was trying to look like a wealthy businessman from one of the *ranchos*. He even wore a top hat without a single dent in it.

Before mounting up in the morning, I washed myself in a little stream trickling through the weeds. Almost at once I saw a tiny gold button shining like a light in the water. Only it wasn't a button. It was a lump of raw gold about the size of a black-eyed pea. My heart sounded like woodpeckers in my ears.

I closed my fingers around the lump, as if to conceal it from Joaquín. But wasn't that the way he'd expect a greedy Yankee to behave? Forget that he'd rescued me from O. O. Mary. Forget that he'd made sure I got food to eat and that he'd brought me to this very spot. The woodpeckers quieted so that I could think, and I opened my fingers.

"Sir, I think I've struck it rich!" I shouted. "Come look!"

He ambled over and picked up the lump. He bounced it in his palm as if to weigh it and then handed it back. He didn't seem very excited. "Don't lose it," he said. "It must be worth ten dollars."

Was that all? "But there must be lots more in this stream."

"There was, *muchacho.* Can't you see the bottles and oyster cans? And the piles of dirt and gravel dumped along the banks? Miners were busy here, eh? They have sifted out the gold. Somehow, that lump of yours got left behind."

"Can't we come back and look for more?"

"When you have time to waste."

"But how will I find this spot? Where are we?"

"Poverty Creek," he said. He took out his knife and carved an *X* on a tall locust tree. "Look for this tree, eh? That will tell you where to stake your claim."

I tore a bit of rag off the tail of my shirt, wrapped up the gold lump, and snugged it in the pillowcase with my other belongings. It was like having money of my own at last. And if these were the gold diggings, Lank might be around the corner somewhere. I'd keep a sharper eye out.

When we mounted up, I tried to fix the tall and lacy locust tree in my mind, and all the surroundings, so I could find my way back. But after twenty minutes the hills and the trees came to appear confoundedly alike.

Not far off we passed Drizzly Gulch. That was too small to suit Joaquín, though it did have a store, some saloons, and a place to eat. Joaquín was looking for a town with a newspaper in it, and we found it a few miles down the road.

"Bedbug," said Joaquín, reading off the sign nailed to a tree. "Correct?"

I could see tin roofs flashing up ahead in the late-afternoon sun. "Is that the name of a town?" I asked. I wasn't sure I wanted to set foot in a place called Bedbug, but at last I knew where I was, kind of.

"You will ride in ahead of me," he said.

His lighthearted smiles vanished. He wrapped one of his pistols in his scarf and handed it to me. "First, you stop in the barbershop and ask if your brother has been seen in Bedbug. The barber hears all the gossip."

I got fairly excited. It surprised me that he cared whether I found my brother or not. It seemed clear that he meant to turn me loose.

"While you are in the barbershop," he went on, "you ask to borrow a couple of newspapers to read to a friend. That friend is me, eh? We will see how good you have taught me to read."

"Reading a cookbook is a good deal different from reading a whole newspaper."

His eyes tightened on me. "And then you go to the newspaper and talk to the editor."

"But why?"

"You tell him that Joaquín and Three-Fingered Jack had a falling-out. You will say that the great outlaw lies dead just off the road. Hand him my scarf and pistol to prove it. Look, I burned my initials in the handle."

I glanced down at the handle. The initials JM stood out like a cattle brand. "And then what?"

Suddenly he was smiling again. "And then, *muchacho*—and then you will claim the reward!"

CHAPTER 8

"I'M A GIRL!"

It was a cunning but wicked scheme. It would amuse him to collect the reward the *gringos* had placed on his own head.

"But, sir," I said, "I don't think anyone's going to hand over the reward money without seeing your body. Your *dead* body, sir."

"I don't think I care to arrange that detail, *muchacho.* Just do as I say."

"And when I do, I hope you will mark my account paid in full."

"What are you talking about, *muchacho*?"

"I've taught you to read, more or less. I've kept my part of the bargain. You will turn me loose. Do I have your promise?"

He looked genuinely stricken. "You have some complaint about the way I treated you?" he asked.

"Of course not," I said.

"You are unhappy?"

"Not exactly. But you are bandits and horse thieves."

"True."

"My mother would turn you in, I think."

"And you?"

I was feeling uncomfortable. How much loyalty did I owe him? "I'll give you a head start," I promised solemnly.

He grinned. "I'll be in town, keeping an eye on you. I may touch my hat to you in the plaza. Once I leave, you go your own way, and good luck, Yankee."

I heaved a sigh of relief. "Good-bye, sir."

And I rode alone into Bedbug. Just the name began giving me the all-over itches, and I began to scratch whether I needed to or not. There hardly seemed room in town for anything but saloons, but I spied out the barbershop behind a cloud of flies. I also spied out a wanted poster tacked to the front of a building I took to be a jail. Joaquín was wanted in Bedbug, as he was everywhere else.

I tied the buckskin to the hitch rail outside the

barbershop. The barber, who wore a starched collar, was waxing the ends of his mustache at the wall mirror. The ends curved around, sharp as fishhooks.

"Sir," I said, "I'm looking for my brother, Lankly Lafayette Smith. He's somewhere in the gold diggings. Have you heard any word about him? He's tall for his age and still growing—he's seventeen, though he'll be eighteen in March. He has green eyes like mine and hair down to his shoulders the last time I saw him."

"Ain't laid eyes on him," said the barber.

"Are you sure?"

"If he turns up, I'll tell him you was looking for him."

"I'll be obliged," I said.

"Want your hair cut? I'll only charge you a nickel."

"I'm letting my hair grow out," I said. "Do you have any old newspapers I could have?"

"Sonny, we read 'em until the print's wore out. And then we use 'em for wallpaper."

I wasn't too crestfallen that he'd never heard of my brother, for I felt I was getting off to a start at last. As I was about to cross the street to the newspaper office, I saw Joaquín ride slowly into town. He pretended he didn't know me.

A little overhead bell jangled when I opened the door of the newspaper office.

"Are you the editor?" I asked a fuzzy-bearded man at a cubbyhole desk. He was wearing a broken-down hat squarely on his head, like a tree stump.

"I'm the editor, publisher, janitor, and everything else around here," he said. His name turned out to be Yellow Bird Ridge and he was half Cherokee Indian. "Lad, how would you like to own this misbegotten rag of a newspaper? I'll listen to a reasonable offer. Or even an unreasonable offer. I might trade the whole shebang for your jackknife."

"No, sir," I said. "I just came to hand over this pistol and this scarf."

"I am not in need of either, young feller."

"They belonged to Joaquín Muricta."

He jumped as if he'd discovered a ball of lightning on the seat of his chair. His hat seemed to rise off his head. "Not truly!"

"Truly," I said solemnly. "You can see his initials on the handle."

"So I can. Are you trying to tell me that Joaquín the Terrible is dead?"

I wanted to be careful to tell the truth as best I could yet keep my word to Joaquín. "Dead, sir? Well, I didn't feel his heart to see if it had stopped beating."

"You took this scarf and pistol off him?"

"He didn't seem to want them anymore."

"Where'd the great villain fall?" asked Mr. Yellow Bird Ridge.

"He didn't fall exactly. His last words to me were that he'd a falling-out with Three-Fingered Jack. But that might not be the exact truth."

"Shot by Three-Fingered Jack!" The editor had now jerked himself to his feet. As if the story couldn't wait another moment, he tightened the hat on his head and began setting big pieces of wooden type with his fingers. "This'll be the greatest news to hit California since gold was discovered at Sutter's sawmill."

"Yes, sir," I said.

"How do you like the sound of this for my headline? TERRIBLE JOAQUÍN, THE ROBIN HOOD OF THE MOUNTAINS, DEAD IN A BLAZE OF GUNFIRE."

"Robin Hood?" I muttered doubtfully. "Didn't he steal from the king mostly? I hear that Joaquín steals from anybody, sir."

"Of course! The bandit has learned about democracy. So he steals from everyone equally. Oh, I know a bookful about the Terrible Joaquín. Now that the rascal's dead, I might write it."

The Robin Hood of the Mountains? The words began to glow in my head. They made him seem like a bigger splash than a common horse thief and outlaw. They made him seem kind of exalted. And it was true he helped his people.

But how true was true? Wasn't Joaquín still a terrible villain? A murderer even? My mother would be glad to be shed of such company, and I should be, too.

I heard the newspaperman say, "You're after the reward, of course. What's your name?"

"The reward? No, sir," I said. "I don't want a penny of it."

He was so busy setting type that he didn't seem to be paying close attention. "Don't count your chickens before they're hatched, lad—or your bandits, either. There are lots of Joaquíns in California. Someone who knew the real gent will have to identify the body."

With a flash that took my breath away, I suddenly saw that Joaquín wasn't after the reward money. He was up to some hanky-panky of his own. He meant to draw that villain Calico out of hiding. It was Calico who, face-to-face, had once tied Joaquín to a tree. Calico would be anxious to identify the dead outlaw!

"Now, where'd you leave the body?" asked the editor.

"I left him on the road over in that direction," I said, pointing, and that was the truth. "Can I have an old newspaper?"

"Help yourself."

I folded up a newspaper and stuffed it in my pillow slip.

"How many bullet holes in the body?" he asked.

"I didn't count, sir."

"Six. I've never known Three-Fingered Jack to fire fewer than six bullets even at a tin can."

"Suit yourself," I said.

Mr. Yellow Bird Ridge looked over from his type-case, "What did you say your name was?"

"Annyrose Smith," I said, feeling suddenly light-hearted. If newspapers all around picked up the story, as they were bound to, Lank would be sure to read my name. "Annyrose Smith of Vermilion Parish, Louisiana," I said. "Make sure you put that in."

The editor was staring at me. "Annyrose is a girl's name."

"I'm a girl!" I declared.

CHAPTER 9

THE CITIZENS OF BEDBUG

I'd kept my bargain with Joaquín and suddenly felt as free as the wind. I walked into the general store, put my lump of gold on the counter, and walked out in a pink gingham dress, a white bonnet, and a pair of girl shoes fresh out of the shoe barrel.

Joaquín, ambling along the boardwalk, didn't recognize me. That's when I noticed four or five men standing around the no-name buckskin I had tied outside the barbershop.

"That pony is stolen!" I heard a tall man shout. "It looks like my nephew's long-haired buckskin down in Santa Barbara. I'd know it anywhere! Look at the brand!"

Everyone clustered around to look at the brand. The

barber had come out to see what all the fuss was about. "Maybe there's a cross brand," he said. "Your nephew might have sold the horse."

I found myself backing into a doorway; it turned out to be the doorway of the sheriff's office. I should have had better sense than to ride the buckskin into town. It didn't surprise me that someone recognized the horse. It was just the sort of evil luck that had my name all over it.

The men checked the left shoulder of the buckskin. There was no second brand, as I guessed there would have been if the horse had been sold fair and square.

"It's stolen, sure as a goose goes barefoot!"

"That's a hangin' crime! Anybody seen who rode the horse and tied it up?"

The barber cleared his voice. "It was a skinny boy with turned-up boots. A polite little feller. He didn't look like a horse thief."

"They never do," someone said.

"Let's find him and string him up," someone else called out.

"You're going to hang a boy?"

"Man or boy, a horse thief is a horse thief!"

My heart was stuck in my throat. I managed to force myself out of the sheriff's doorway. As I edged past the saloon next door, I glimpsed Joaquín inside gambling at faro or some other squalid game. As I passed the window, I caught sight of a girl in a pink gingham dress and a bonnet: me. Me, a girl! Hallelujah! I thought. The men would be scouring the town for a boy.

I was finally able to take a full breath. I began to walk slowly, chin up, along the warped boardwalk toward the end of town and the scrubby trees. Then I came to my senses. How long would it be before the man in the general store remembered the boy who'd plunked down a lump of gold and walked out dressed in pink?

I didn't even reach the edge of town when the men were buzzing around me like a swarm of hornets. They hadn't even bothered to mount their horses.

"Hang her!"

"We can't hang a girl!"

"Why not?"

"It don't seem polite."

"We hang horse thieves, don't we?"

A hairy man, big as a haystack, held up his hand. "Don't be hasty. We'll hold her in jail until the sheriff gets back."

At least someone had good sense and a cool head,

SALOON

I thought, and a flash of hope shot through me. But hope faded quickly as the big man was drowned out by fresh shouts to get a long rope.

"Gents, you are correct. A horse thief should be strung up on the spot! But a child?"

That last voice I could have recognized in a howling wind. It was Joaquín himself, astride his black, long-tailed horse. Top hat and all, he looked as stern as a judge.

He announced, "I am Dr. Hidalgo Martínez Feliz Álvarado de Cardoza of Madrid, Spain, where we do not hang children! If you wish to hang this girl, you will have to hang me first!"

The next thing I knew he'd caught me in his arm as if it were a shepherd's hook. He kicked his spurs. I held on, and off we flew. Finally Joaquín swung me up behind him. The last backward glimpse I had of Bedbug was when Yellow Bird Ridge stepped out of the door of his newspaper office to see what was going on. He looked as if he were rattling mad for being distracted from the great story he was writing about the death of Joaquín Murieta.

CHAPTER 10

THE THIRD FIDDLER

If Bedbug mounted up to chase after us, we saw neither hide nor hair of a posse. We'd got a fair head start, and Joaquín's horse was swift and powerful. For all I know, the men had got second thoughts about hanging a child and had no heart for the chase.

"So you're a girl," said Joaquín finally. I was riding behind him, hanging on to the sash under his coat where he stuck his pistols and knife. I couldn't tell whether he was angry or bemused. After all, I had hoaxed him, and it wouldn't surprise me if he had shot men for less.

"You almost got me hanged!" I exclaimed.

"Would that be such a great loss?"

"It would be to me!"

"*Gringo!* You didn't even thank me for saving your life."

"Don't call me *gringo.* My name is Annyrose. Of course, I thank you."

"Declared with such enthusiasm! I may not bother next time."

What next time? "If this horse of yours is stolen," I said, "I'd prefer to walk, sir."

He gave out a whispered snarl and hauled up on the reins. "Then walk, *muchacha*! Girl!"

I slipped to the ground. Off he rode, the horse's hooves flinging back dirt in my face.

Looking around, I realized I was abandoned in the middle of nowhere, with no money and nothing to eat. I felt a great need to burst into tears, but I held back all but a drop or two.

I trudged along the trail in my new shoes. They needed breaking in and hurt my feet. I was bound to come to a town somewhere on this road, I told myself, unless I died of starvation first. But after two hours there seemed to be no end to the trees, and it would soon be dark. I was beginning to feel a little scared. There were bound to be bears in these woods.

I found a patch of wild berries on prickly vines, and I went at them with both hands. When I returned to the road, my arms looked as if they'd been separating snarling cats.

It fell dark, and I thought I'd climb a tree for the night. But bears climbed trees, didn't they?

I kept walking until long after dark. By then I was so tired I didn't care whether a bear ate me or not. I gathered up some fresh-smelling pine needles for a bed and fell asleep.

When I awoke in the morning, there stood Joaquín waiting for my eyes to open.

"I bought you a horse," he declared.

"What?"

"*Sí,* with my winnings at faro. Look. Here's the bill of sale! See for yourself! It's true, no?"

I didn't ask any more questions. I looked at the horse, spotted as if he had kicked over a barrel of whitewash, and I smiled good and wide. I climbed into the saddle and patted his shoulder to get acquainted. Joaquín adjusted the stirrups so my feet could reach them, and we rode away.

"Are there bears in these woods?" I asked.

"Of course," said the bandit. "But you're too full of thorns to eat."

I couldn't exactly figure out why he took the trouble to look after me. Did he need to show that he wasn't as low-down and heartless as the Yankee thought? I wondered what sort of man he would have been now if he hadn't been so cruelly wronged.

And now I had been wronged. It would be a wonder if I didn't turn up on a wanted poster as a confounded eleven-year-old horse thief.

For reasons of his own, Joaquín didn't seem to be heading back for the hideout. We avoided the towns, more or less, and again traveled mostly at night. Now that he was supposed to be dead, I guessed that he didn't want to risk being recognized even dressed up in high-and-mighty clothes.

The spotted horse, I quickly discovered, had an easy gait and a smooth trot. "Does this animal have a name?" I asked.

"He's smart. Ask him."

"Ha," I said. "Maybe I'll name him after I get to know him better."

Now that we had a newspaper, Joaquín didn't let a day pass without attempting to read it. There was a report of the coach holdup I had witnessed on the Mariposa road. It said that a man, as yet unidentified, had been shot. At the same time Joaquín and Three-Fingered Jack were blamed for killing four Yankees, one Frenchman, and seven Chinese in Calaveras, Hangtown, and San Jose.

The outlaw gave a bemused shrug. "How can Joaquín be in so many places at once, eh? And ride with you, peaceful as a rabbit, at the same time?"

He sent me into Jackson with a few pinches of gold dust for food to bring back. I stuck my head in the barbershop to see if I could turn up any news of my brother. All that my questions produced were a couple of shrugs. I heard no one talking about the demise of the great outlaw, so it was clear that the news hadn't yet traveled this far. I was able to buy half a loaf of bread, some dried peaches, and two cans of sardines.

I was riding back when I saw two whiskered miners in front of their split-board shanty, seated at waxed music stands and playing fiddles. I stopped and sat on my horse and listened. The music thrilled me. I thought it must be a Beethoven duet they were playing. Or was it Haydn? For the first time I realized how desperately I missed my instrument.

The miners turned out to be professors of music from Boston who'd run off to the gold rush. They couldn't help noticing that they had an audience and seemed to play with a little more fire. When they came to the end, one of them gave me a welcoming wave of his bow.

"Stay awhile. You like Mozart?"

"Is that who you were playing?"

"No doubt it sounded somewhat lame. It's transcribed for three instruments, but there are only two of us."

"I used to play the violin," I said.

Their hairy faces burst into smiles. "I'm Seth Partridge, and this is my brother, Dana. Stay awhile and sit in with us."

"I'm not that good at it, sir."

"You can read the notes, can't you?"

"Of course."

"That'll be good enough. Take my fiddle. I've got a viola. We'll try a little Schubert."

The moment I clutched his polished violin under my chin, there came a rush of memories of home and Papa teaching me to play. But I hardly had time to spring a tear when the brothers were off and running and turning pages. It was all I could do to keep up. My playing sounded as thin as skim milk to me, but the brothers hardly seemed to notice. When we finished, I felt as exhilarated as if I'd climbed a mountain and slid all the way down the other side.

I handed back the violin and hopped up to leave. "Rest a bit," said Seth. "Dana, fetch some refreshment."

I said, "I've got to get back." I didn't want Joaquín worrying about me.

The younger brother hurriedly brought out a Mexican basket with pomegranates. So I stayed a little longer, and Dana said, "I hope you're moving onto our mountain. A trio sounds so much better played by three, don't you agree?"

"No, sir, and yes, sir," I said. "We're moving on, my friend and I."

Seth frowned, "Well, if you don't move too far, we'll pay you in a couple of pinches of gold dust to sit in with us when you can. Isn't that right, Dana?"

"And double when there are a lot of grace notes."

I wondered if I could take care of myself with pinches of gold dust. But that was out of the question for now. Joaquín was waiting for something to eat.

I asked suddenly, "Aren't you afraid that the Mexican bandit will steal your gold?"

"Joaquín? He has no reason to harm us."

"You are Yankees."

"Some Yankees are no-account," continued the older brother. "We all get tarred with the same brush."

Certainly O. O. Mary was one of the no-accounts, I thought. "It's not true, is it, that we passed laws against Mexicans?" I asked. I hoped that I had been told a tale.

"Oh, it's true," said Seth. "When there was plenty of gold, everyone worked cheek by jowl. Indians, Chinese, Mexicans. But once the pickings thinned out, some miners turned greedy as pigs for what was left. They got the politicians to pass some mangy laws. Trash sometimes rises to the top, miss."

"But we have overturned those laws," added Dana.

"And hardly a moment too soon," said Seth.

"Then Mexicans can do as they please?" I exclaimed.

"Of course."

The information cheered me. Didn't Joaquín know? I could hardly wait to tell him.

I picked at the pomegranate seeds, each buried in a ruby sack, tart and juicy. When I finished, my fingers were stained red.

The first thing Joaquín said to me when I returned was: "Ah, you have found a pomegranate."

I fairly shouted out, "Did you know that the laws against your people were changed?"

"Of course."

"You knew?"

"I remain insulted."

I looked at him and saw that for the great bandit, nothing was altered. He would continue his proud outlaw life, avenging himself on Yankees. Like an arrow in flight, he couldn't change direction.

CHAPTER 11

I PICK UP LANK'S TRAIL

The stars came out, and we rode on. I stole glances at Joaquín, riding with his chin held high, like an emperor in disguise surveying his domain. He seemed to have friends everywhere, countrymen he trusted, and some nights we slept on small *ranchos,* in regular beds. I was almost forgetting what mattresses felt like.

I'd hear Joaquín and his friends talking, almost in whispers. I figured this was a way Joaquín had of spying on things going in the diggings.

"You don't need to read the newspapers," I said, as if I'd been wasting my time teaching him.

"In my profession, Yankee, one cannot have too many sources of information. And how else would I know what Three-Fingered Jack and the others are up to, eh? The pickings are slim along the roads. I learned that we have acquired a Yankee mule train with three barrels of homemade soap."

"Acquired? Stole, you mean."

"Don't get your fur up, *muchacha.* We'll have to give that soap to the church. I never heard of a miner using it."

I might have laughed at his joke, but I couldn't. Did his outlaws steal just for the sake of stealing, whether it was something they wanted or not? Did they steal only to vex the *gringos*? I was greatly troubled. How much vengeance was enough? Was the rage in his blood never going to burn itself out?

In Dogtown they hadn't seen a newspaper in weeks. And no one seemed to be looking for a child horse thief.

But my heart soon gave a great leap! In the general store the clerk thought he'd sold a wide-brimmed slouch hat to someone answering my brother Lank's description.

And a growing boy in a new, floppy hat had been seen in Butte City. He'd come and gone weeks ago, but I felt that I was getting almost close enough to my brother to touch him.

I lost his trail in Chili Camp, which was hardly

more than canvas tents looking like a sprouting up of mushrooms. It was full of miners from Guatemala and Ecuador and Chile. Joaquín didn't entirely trust the *chilenos,* as he called them, whether they were from Chile or Ecuador or Guatemala. They weren't his countrymen, and he said they'd turn him in for the reward if they had the chance. I was beginning to wonder if it was against the law in the diggings to like anyone who wasn't of the same stripe as you.

I think Joaquín was meeting with one of his spies when I returned to the woods with news from Chili Camp. I heard a horse crashing away through the brush.

"What did you learn?" Joaquín asked, turning to me.

"First," I said like a schoolmarm, "first, you'll notice if you look down the road that the sign on the tree is spelled wrong. Chile, the country, is spelled with an *e* at the end. Second, I saw the impostor, big as life, the man in the road who pretended to be you."

"The fool who tried to hold me up?"

"The same. And still riding that rattleboned horse."

Joaquín absorbed this information with a smile and a shrug. "I trust he won't make a further bother of himself. You have been to Sawmill Flat?"

"Of course not."

"We will go there."

"Third," I said, "I heard a rumor that a big posse has been formed to hunt you down."

A smile swept his face. "Poor fellows!"

CHAPTER 12

THE EVENTS AT SAWMILL FLAT

We wound our way through the shadowy pines and live oaks. I couldn't help noticing that a sharper alertness had settled in Joaquín's eyes. He had the look of a man expecting to step on a rattlesnake at any moment. I don't think it was concern about the new posse. The very air in these hills seemed to threaten him.

Long after the sun went down, we crept silently into the woods above Sawmill Flat and made camp. Joaquín wouldn't light a fire, not even to light one of his twisty cigars.

During the days he gazed down on miners in the stream below. They worked away at their gold pans and long boxes, washing out the earth for treasure.

We could hear their distant voices, but not exactly what they were saying. An adobe house, with what appeared to be a grapevine clutching its way up the south wall, sat on the slope of the hill.

Joaquín sent me into Sonora a few miles away to see if the news of his death had arrived.

Sonora seemed almost a big city after the shantytowns we had been in. But I could pick up no information about Lank, and nobody was jabbering about the happy end of Joaquín Murieta. Because of holdups on the road, I learned, it had been weeks since the newspaper from Stockton had reached Sonora.

During the next two days Joaquín said only a few words to me, and those in a whisper. He was silent as an owl about to take wing and strike.

I grew edgy. Did he mean to murder those innocent men below? Why? Because they were *gringos*? I made up my mind to warn them. But how? A sneeze would carry in the stillness. Wouldn't that let them know there was someone lurking in the woods above them? Joaquín would have a fit.

But when I awoke in the morning, his deed was done. Joaquín had struck in the night and returned with seven rawhide pouches of gold, each the size of a hip pocket.

"You robbed them?" I said.

"Of course, *muchacha*. You didn't notice the big *hombre* in the blue shirt loading up his saddlebag? My spy told me those miners plan to deposit their gold dust in the Wells Fargo vault. I took every ounce without firing a shot."

"But those men worked hard for that gold!"

"True. But see that grapevine? My wife, Carmela, planted it. See the house? I built it. This was my land, *muchacha*, but the Yankee miners jumped my claim. I stole nothing. Can I appear in court to reclaim my land, eh, an outlaw? The gold in these pouches was mine from the beginning. If the *gringos* wish to oblige me by digging it out, I let them."

I peered down the hillside again. I saw a tall pine, straight as a lance, and wondered if that was the tree that the ruffian Calico and his friends had used to hang Joaquín's brother. And it must have been from the earthen adobe below that Calico's men had carried off Carmela.

I now knew why Joaquín's mood had darkened as we approached these hills. For him the ground must still be steaming with brimstone and fire.

We faded away into the mountains, and a few days later Joaquín surprised me by riding boldly into Murphy's Diggings. I had a feeling that he couldn't stand lurking in the shadows any longer. He needed to step out into the footlights and thumb his nose at the Yankees.

No one, after all, would take him for the famous outlaw, all dusted off in a top hat and with an innocent girl in a white bonnet riding beside him. It must have appealed to his thirst for danger.

So there we were on the busy street, tying up our horses outside a butcher shop, when a voice rang out. I saw a finger as long as a stick pointing our way.

"That's him! *Sí! Sí!* That's Joaquín the bandit!"

On his rattleboned horse sat the Chilean impostor.

"Catch him!" he shouted. "The fancy *sombrero* doesn't fool me! Me, I've looked into the eyes of Joaquín himself. *Ay*, that's him! It's Joaquín the bandit! The reward is mine!"

Like an alarm bell, the shouting brought men running toward us with new shouts of their own. "Joaquín! The bandit? There's a thousand dollars on his head! Dead or alive!"

Joaquín tried to leap back onto his saddle, but a miner in a checkered shirt caught his leg and held on like a bear. I hardly had time to catch my breath before the men had Joaquín wrestled to the ground.

The impostor was grinning wildly. "Remember, *hombres*, I saw him first! *Sí*, the reward is mine!"

I can't explain my sudden blind fury. How dare this bumbling clod denounce Joaquín, who had spared his life? I was astonished to hear my own voice rising above the others.

"You are mistaken, sir! Your only reward will be if this gentleman spares your life—again!"

The miners had disarmed Joaquín of his pistols and knife and dragged him back to his feet. I was surprised at how small he looked among them.

An oaf in the crowd, who seemed to be all heavy shoulders and narrow eyes, declared, "Yup, he's a greaser, just like Joaquín! Must be him!"

"If you mean he's Mexican, it's true," I shouted. "But he's entitled to be tried by a court of law, not hanged by a mob in the street!"

Joaquín threw me a baffled glance. What was I yelling about? Didn't I know that he'd been in tighter spots than this? He could take care of himself.

But I couldn't stop shouting. "He's an educated man. Joaquín the bandit cannot even sign his own name. Look at this!"

I made a dive for the pillowcase tied to my saddle horn and pulled out the book.

"Here's my mother's cookbook!" I said, and held it up for all to see. "Could Joaquín the bandit read it? Of course not! *Señor!* Read a page for the edification of these men."

A blacksmith in his leather apron took the book from me and held it in front of Joaquín's face—upside down.

I took it out of his hands, righted the book, and held it up myself. "*Señor*, what does this page say?"

"Of course, daughter," said Joaquín with all the grace and airs of a stage actor. He seemed pleased with my quick thinking. He read, in a loud voice, as if hatched by Shakespeare himself, " 'Herring Pie'!"

"What in tarnation's herring pie?" someone asked.

Said Joaquín, "You call yourself civilized, sir, and you've never dined on herring pie?"

"I've eaten my weight in it," said a man with a New England accent.

"Read on," commanded the blacksmith.

" 'Take white pickled herrings,' " Joaquín declared, for he knew the words by heart. " 'Boil them a little, remove the skin, keep the backs only and remove the bones. Put them in a pastry casing—' "

"That'll do," said a white-haired man, who turned out to be the local printer. He screwed up his eyes to glance at the printed page. "That's what the book says, word for word. Boys, you owe this gent an apology. Give him back his guns."

A smile broke across Joaquín's face. *"Es destino,"* he said to me in a soft whisper. "There was nothing to fear, daughter. It will be my destiny to hang from the limb of an oak tree. You see the hanging tree at the end of the street? It is not an oak."

"And another thing," the white-haired printer was saying. "The newspaper's just in from Stockton. Joaquín the bandit will disturb the peace no more. The rascal is dead!"

CHAPTER 13

THE MAN ON THE ROAD

The crowd treated the news as if it were the Fourth of July, shooting off guns in the air and yelling and whooping and dancing in the street. In all the noise and confusion the Chilean impostor vanished. I was angry with Joaquín for stupidly exposing himself to needless danger and making my heart leap up into my throat. He had no business riding, big as life, into Murphy's Diggings.

"But it was my business, daughter, to show a Mexican face. Here miners once threw us off the streets."

"But not now."

A smile flickered across his face. "Can you imagine? The law proved to be against the law."

"Who changed it? Yankees?"

"I didn't ask."

"Of course, Yankees. Perhaps some of the very men you have held up on the roads."

"Then, daughter, they should wear signs around their necks saying, 'I am a good Yankee.' The next thing, you will be telling me that not all Mexicans are bandits."

"Of course not. That's nonsense. And don't call me daughter."

"Then why do you talk to me like one?"

He had me buy a copy of the Stockton newspaper and rode out of Murphy's Diggings with his head held high. I rode beside him, feeling very confused. He ought to have been offended that men were dancing in the street as if it were his grave, but he wasn't. The miners treated him like an outlaw because he *was* an outlaw. I had treated him like a friend, rushing in to save his neck, but how could an outlaw be my friend?

"Read the newspaper, *muchacha*," he said. "What does it say about me?"

"You can read it for yourself, sir," I said, in a flinty voice barely above a whisper.

He gave me a sharp look. "Something is eating you? You want to go your own way? Go. Didn't I thank you for trying to save my life?"

"You don't have to thank me."

"You showed a quick wit. *Magnífico.*"

"Where does this road lead?" I asked.

"Angels Camp."

"I'll leave you there."

"Give me the newspaper," he declared, as if I hadn't said anything of the slightest importance to him. Maybe he didn't believe me.

As we rode along, he unfolded the newspaper and had some trouble reading the headline in big letters as black as shoe polish.

JOAQUÍN IS DEAD!
GREAT JUBILATION!

He held the paper for me to see. "What is this word?"

"*Jubilation,*" I said. "You could have ciphered it out, sir."

"What does it mean?"

"Happiness."

"I am glad to make people feel happy. And this word?"

"Feverish."

He read on, stumbling along in a full voice. " 'Our county has been thrown into a feverish state of excitement at the news, just arrived from Bedbug, that the daring and fiery bandit Joaquín Murieta has been put to bed with a shovel! The notorious highwayman was shot full of holes. In a falling out between thieves, Three-Fingered Jack fired away point-blank. Joaquín's own heavy Colt pistol with his initials carved in it and his bloody red scarf have been recovered and are in the hands of the sheriff there. The lawman declared them to be authentic.' "

He'd begun galloping over the story, smiling, laughing, and impatiently leaping words that resisted him. I could fill them in for myself. I took a moment's pride in how quickly he'd learned to puzzle out printed words. I'd done what I promised to do.

He kept reading. " 'The body was discovered by a young girl named Annyrose Smith, of parts unknown. A search party has been sent out to bring back the body, and it will be measured for a wooden overcoat.

" 'Once the body can be identified for certain, the thousand-dollar reward will be forthcoming. The girl herself has wisely disappeared, rescued by a stranger from Madrid. Hotheads almost hanged her by mistake as a horse thief. It was clear that the stolen horse she rode into Bedbug had been in the possession of the dead outlaw.'

"*Bueno,*" Joaquín muttered, a fresh smile glowing up like a sunrise. "Good. Perhaps at this very moment

Señor Calico is reading these words and will invite himself to the funeral."

And I thought that at any moment Lank might be reading my name and be heading for Bedbug to find me.

"Sir, if I follow this road, will it take me back to Bedbug?" I asked.

"Only if you know where to turn off."

"Do you think that that awful man Calico will head for Bedbug?"

He nodded.

"Is that where you're going?"

"It's possible, *muchacha*."

I cleared my throat. "Maybe I'll come along that far."

"But you have tired of the company of Joaquín Murieta."

"I didn't say I had tired of your company. I just said I'd be leaving. Every time we meet someone on the road, I have a fear you're going to hold him up."

I'd already noticed the horseman approaching through the trees. He had the muddy boots of a miner and whiskers as stiff as pine needles. He was bound to have a pouch or two of gold dust on him, I thought. I gave Joaquín a quick and apprehensive look.

As if to make a liar of my thoughts, Joaquín touched

his hatbrim in a kind of friendly salute. "Howdy, stranger," he said, mimicking a Yankee voice. "Are we safe from bandits on this road?"

"Reckon so," said the miner. "I hear that Joaquín has been shot up like a sardine can. He's deader'n a moldy fig."

"And about time!" exclaimed Joaquín with a great sigh of relief.

"Now," said the miner, revealing a long pistol in his hand. "If you'll just toss over your valuables, I'll let you go on your way."

"My stars," said Joaquín, still in his Yankee voice, "you're nothing but a common bandit!"

"Common as dirt. Let's see your gold fast, or I'll fire at that child."

"That won't be necessary, Yankee."

I caught a mere flash of puckered worry in Joaquín's eyes—not for himself, I thought. For me.

Joaquín jerked back on his reins, and about six things seemed to happen at once. His horse reared up and danced around on his hind legs. The thief found himself looking up at a ton of horseflesh hovering over him. Joaquín managed to whip my horse's rump, and I went galloping down the road, safely out of the way. As I looked back, I saw him kick a big spur into the flank of the miner's horse. The animal bolted. Joaquín peppered the air with a few pistol shots, and the highwayman decided to keep going.

When Joaquín caught up with me, he said, "Next time, *muchacha,* dodge behind me. Don't allow yourself to be such an easy target."

"Would he really have fired at me?"

"For certain. A thief like that gives us outlaws a bad name."

I silently thanked Joaquín for saving me from a gunshot wound or worse. When I looked back, the highwayman had vanished over the hill. I was sure he hadn't a notion how heads-or-tails lucky he was. If I hadn't been along, I'm sure Joaquín would have left *him* as dead as a moldy fig.

CHAPTER 14

DREADFUL NEWS

It was night when we reached Angels Camp. The sloping main street was lit with kerosene lanterns and a couple of flaming torches. People were everywhere, roaming in and out of the shops and saloons. Joaquín read off the signs, dazzled and beaming with pleasure at his new skill. He stumbled a bit over ANGELS APOTHECARY SHOP, but so did I. It turned out to be a place to buy medicine.

We ate dinner in a ramshackle restaurant, and I suddenly saw Pio Pio looking in the window.

Joaquín motioned him inside. "Did you have trouble finding me, eh, Pio?"

He spoke in a whisper. "Not much. You have friends everywhere, *patrón.*"

That may be so, I thought, but it surprised me how boldly Joaquín in a tall hat could ride through the foothills without being recognized—except by accident. The miners no more knew what he looked like than the artist who'd drawn his picture for the wanted posters. And I'd already seen three of those posters nailed up in Angels Camp.

"Sit down and eat," said Joaquín.

The last time Pio Pio saw me I was in breeches and suspenders. He didn't recognize me in a dress and bonnet.

"*Patrón*, I can't talk to you before strangers."

Joaquín laughed. "Talk your head off. This is the Yankee who traveled with us from San Diego."

"The schoolteacher? A boy, no?"

"The girl schoolteacher. *Sí*, in the clothes of somebody else. She saved my life."

Pio Pio's eyes blinked wide open and stared at me.

"Hello, *amigo*," I said. It surprised me how glad I was to see him. I had hardly laid eyes on anyone else in the diggings near my own age. "My name's really Annyrose."

"I am Pio Pio," he muttered.

"I know who you are. We don't have to be introduced all over again."

He gave a little grin and finally sat down. "Three-Fingered Jack sent me to warn you, *patrón*. A new posse is forming to track you down."

"Still another posse? They're like dogs chasing their own tails."

"But this one is different, *señor*. The governor himself signed the order! They are called Ranger, these men, and Three-Fingered Jack says their leader is almost as mean and cold-hearted as Three-Fingered Jack himself. He's from Texas, their leader, and fought us in the war. His name is Captain Harry Love."

Joaquín seemed more interested in the Dutch pancakes he was eating than in the new posse. "But this Captain Love is too late, eh? He must have seen in the newspapers that the great Mexican bandit is no more."

Pio Pio shook his head. "They've searched the roads out of Bedbug and can't find your bones."

"They will keep looking."

"Three-Fingered Jack said the posse suspects a trick. They are sniffing your trail like a pack of hounds."

"The captain will earn my respect—if he catches me! Any news of that dog Calico?"

"Only that Manuel, the saddlemaker, saw him in a coach heading north from Fresno."

"When?"

"Just two days ago."

Joaquín sat back and smiled. *"Bueno."*

Pio Pio rode with us through Cherokee Flat and across a river jammed over with miners and barking dogs. Joaquín led us down through the foothills. I was glad to have Pio Pio to talk to.

We had lagged behind when I said, "You're good with horses. And you know how to live off the land, Pio Pio. But don't you want to get some learning and make something of yourself?"

"Of course I want to make something of myself. I told you. I want to be like Joaquín."

"That's not a worthy ambition."

"It is for me."

"Bah," I said.

"Will your books teach me how to be a great bandit?"

"Of course not."

"Then keep them."

After a while he said, "What about you?"

"What about me what?"

"When you grow up."

"I might be a musician," I said. "I know where I can get a job playing the violin. I used to have one, but O. O. Mary sold it."

"Would you like me to steal one for you?"

"Absolutely not," I answered. "I certainly don't want to advance your career as a bandit."

Toward nightfall I recognized some locust trees off in the distance and I turned to Joaquín. "Isn't that Poverty Creek, where I found my lump of gold?"

"It is," he said.

Then Bedbug couldn't be many miles farther on, I thought. I was certain I'd find Lank there waiting for me, and the expectation filled me with excitement. We came upon a shanty under some willows belonging to a sheep rancher named Carillo.

"We will spend the night with friends," Joaquín said.

"You only just missed Three-Fingered Jack and the others," said the sheepman.

The walls of the shanty had been freshly papered with newspapers. After dinner Joaquín couldn't resist showing off. He picked up a lantern and looked for his name on the walls. "Here I am," he said, touching a newspaper heading with a finger. "And here I am again. What would the newspapers do without me, eh? Look, here is the coach we robbed on the Mariposa road. Remember, when you were sick and your coughing almost gave us away? It says the noisy *hombre* who got himself killed was a gambler and a pickpocket. We did the Yankees a service!"

I didn't know anyone had got killed during the holdup! It horrified me. Why hadn't I coughed louder? I didn't care for gamblers and pickpockets, but I cared heaps less for cold-blooded murder.

I was drawn to the newspaper the next morning just before we left. Did it say that Joaquín had killed the man? As I read, my breath stopped. My head began to swim. "Shot full of holes in the holdup was a gambler and pickpocket identified as Lankly Lafayette Smith, of Vermilion Parish, Louisiana."

CHAPTER 15

"I WANT TO CLAIM THE REWARD"

I stood frozen. The newspaper was wrong. It must be! Lank was no gambler. And he was no pickpocket. The article had got things horribly tangled up.

"Vamos!" Joaquín was calling me. "Let's go!"

But how had the newspaper got Lank's name so exactly right? He must have been riding in that coach. And he must have been the one shot dead. I was hardly fifty yards away when I heard the guns firing. Of course Joaquín had done it!

"Vamos, Yankee!"

I should have burst into tears, but I was too shot through with anger and sudden hatred. I had been riding all over creation beside the man who had killed my brother!

I steeled myself. I didn't say a word as we mounted up, Joaquín and Pio Pio and I. I didn't say a word all morning long. By the time we rode into Drizzly Gulch, I'd made up my mind what I was going to do.

"There's a chowchow shop across the way," said Joaquín, pointing to a small Chinese restaurant with iron shutters. "We'll eat."

"I'm not hungry," I said, looking away. Eat with this villain again? Never!

He shifted his gaze to me. "You sick, Yankee?"

I shook my head. "I'll look in the store window."

I was sorry I said that, for he broke into an understanding smile. "A new dress? That's what you are starved for, eh?"

"No," I protested.

As we dismounted, he tossed me a pouch of gold dust. "Buy whatever pleases you. Come along, Pio Pio."

Off they strode through the iron door of the restaurant. And there I stood in the sun, the gold feeling as hot in my hand as if the devil himself had tossed it to me. I despised the bandit's generosity. But if I flung it back, he'd know something was brewing in my head.

So I tied the gold sack up in the pillow slip with

my other valuables. I left the spotted horse and hurried down the street until I found the sheriff's office. A large blue-eyed man was sitting in a bentwood chair under the wooden awning out front.

"You the sheriff?" I asked breathlessly.

"Yes, missy. Sheriff Elwood Flint. Folks call me Iron Eyes. You can, too."

"I don't see any badge."

"Some feller stole it."

That hardly filled me with confidence. But his eyes did have a steely look, and maybe he'd show the necessary grit. He'd have to do.

"Do you have a jailhouse?" I asked.

"We use the one over in Bedbug."

"Are the walls good and solid?"

"Stones a foot thick," he answered, and coughed out a small laugh. "Who do you want me to lock up? Joaquín Murieta himself?"

"I want to claim the reward," I said. My heart was beating like a ratchet, and my voice came out shaky.

"What reward?"

I took a deep breath, all the way up from my toes. "The reward for the capture of Joaquín, the famous bandit. Yes, Joaquín Murieta himself."

"You're a mite late, missy. That rascal's dead and buried."

"No, he's not! He's sitting right up the street in the chowchow shop. You can't miss him. He's wearing a tall hat. You'd better get up a posse."

"I won't need a posse."

"He'll be too clever for you, sir!"

"That remains to be seen, don't it? You sure it's him?"

"Of course I'm sure."

"It could be some other Joaquín."

"It's not."

"That name's common as fleas around these hills," he said with a snort.

"It's the genuine Joaquín I'm turning in, sir! No mistake about it. My name's Annyrose Smith. Take that down, sir. I don't want any mistake about the reward money."

"Well," said Sheriff Iron Eyes Flint, bestirring himself, "I'll just amble up that way and catch him by surprise and march him off to the hoosegow. Of course we'll have to share the reward, you and me."

I was in no state to argue about it. There'd be enough left over to give my brother a decent burial.

"Agreed?" he said.

"Agreed," I said.

He spit out a wad of tobacco. "I seen a posse of Rangers scouting around these parts. The joke'll be on them if I steal that big Mexican fish right out from under their noses."

I waited until he finished chuckling at the glory. Then I asked, "How far off is Bedbug, sir?"

"Just over that hill and down the road."

I set off on foot. I wouldn't ride that spotted horse Joaquín had given me. I no longer wanted it. I ran for a while, and my eyes began to swim. I didn't care to be close enough to hear any gunshots.

Joaquín deserved what he would get at the hands of the law. But it left me with a sick feeling to have betrayed someone who trusted me. Did that make me no-account and trashy, like O. O. Mary? She'd do a thing like that.

I tried not to think about Pio Pio. He looked too young to be an outlaw, and I hoped Sheriff Elwood Flint would just let him go.

It frightened me to show my face in Bedbug. Someone might recognize me and try all over again to hang me for a horse thief. But I needed to explain and apologize to the man at the newspaper for deceiving him. So in I went, my tears wiped and drying.

The editor was at his desk, just as I'd left him, with the tree stump hat square on his head. His bushy beard looked a little longer and even more tangled.

"Mr. Yellow Bird Ridge," I said, "maybe you remember me. I didn't steal the buckskin horse, sir. But that story I told about Joaquín being shot full of holes, that was hogwash."

He looked at me, picked up his glasses, and looked again. "You should be tarred and feathered."

"I know it, sir."

"Were the bandit's gun and scarf you left with me hoaxes, too?"

"No, sir." I said. "They were his. He said to give them to you."

Amazement sprang up in his eyes. "You know Joaquín Murieta? In person? The honest truth, girl?"

I nodded. "I've been traveling with him."

"And Three-Fingered Jack?"

"Murderers, both of them!"

He sharpened a pencil and hustled up paper to make notes. "Dear child, you must tell me all you know. What color are his eyes? Is he six foot tall? Have you ever seen him laugh? Do you know for a fact how he was wronged? And what was that name of yours?"

"Annyrose Smith."

"Of course it is. Someone dropped off a letter for you a couple of days ago."

Who could be writing me when I didn't know a

soul? Mr. Yellow Bird Ridge dug around in the stuffed cubbyholes of his desk and came out with an envelope sealed with a dab of red wax. I tore it open.

> My dear Sister,
>
> I have found you at last! Remain in Bedbug. I will return for you as soon as we finish this nasty business with the bandit Joaquín Murieta. I have joined the Rangers under Captain Love to track the ruffian down. They are paying me $150 a month. I enclose $10 for your keep until I see you again.
>
> Your devoted brother,
>
> Lank

My head spun! My knees about buckled under me. This didn't read like a letter he'd written before his death. Hardly able to believe my eyes, I studied the date. Lank was alive! I didn't know how, but he was alive. The gambler who was killed certainly wasn't my brother. I stared at the date again. He had written this note only days before.

I must have let out a thunderclap of surprise, for Mr. Yellow Bird Ridge looked up as if I were having sudden fits.

"Was the man who left this letter tall and loose-jointed and yellow-haired?" I cried out.

"I believe he was."

"That was my brother, Lank! Joaquín didn't shoot him dead at all. You were mistaken, sir!"

Suddenly I must have gone white as cotton. What had I done? What would Joaquín think when he discovered I'd turned him in for the reward?

I flew out the door.

CHAPTER 16

A PINCH OF GOLD

I took off my shoes and ran all the way back to Drizzly Gulch. I ducked behind some tall weeds when I saw the street full of men yelling outside the jail. And more were coming.

"Let's see what he looks like!"

"Hang him!"

"Did he shoot the sheriff?"

"Not a shot fired."

And there came the sheriff out on the porch.

"Don't stand around here, boys. There ain't going to be a mob hanging. The reward's spoke for. So git."

No one made a move to leave, and more men were drawn to the excitement. Someone yelled out, "The reward says for the head of Joaquín. It doesn't say you've got to turn him in alive and kicking."

"Read the poster for yourself, Sheriff. No reason we can't hang him."

"Archy's right!"

Another man in a big hat yelled out, "Hold on! Has he ever been tried in a court of law? I think not."

"We'll hold court right here!"

My heart was stuck in my throat. These men were looking for excitement, and their mood was getting meaner and uglier. They would end up dragging him out of the sheriff's office and over to a tree.

There was an old glass jar at my feet. I emptied Joaquín's pouch of gold dust into it and jumped up and rushed out into the street.

"Sir! Sirs! Where's the assay office? Where's the bank! Look at this! Have you ever seen prettier color?" I took a pinch of gold and tossed it into the air as if I'd lost my wits. "Heaps more where that came from!"

"You get that around here?" asked a man in a green vest.

"Not far," I said.

Other miners lifted their noses as if they could smell the gold. They left the mob in ones and twos and came over to gaze into the golden jar.

"Don't it look pure!"

"Kind of lumpy, too!"

A wrinkled man gave a little giggle. "I don't suppose you'd care to tell us where you made your strike, little girl?"

He took me for a bona fide idiot. "It's a secret," I said. And then I gave a little dance and tossed another pinch of gold dust in the air. "But my arms are about worn off digging. If you'll promise to cut me in partners, fifty-fifty, I'll tell you where to dig."

By then about everybody was gathering around me. Gold fever swamped the hanging fever. To a man they shouted promises to go partners with me. So I told them to follow Poverty Creek to some tall locust trees, one in particular, with an *X* carved in the bark. "That's where I hit it lucky," I added. That was true.

The gold rush didn't take a minute to clear the street. Horses rattled out of town as if the ground were afire.

The sheriff found himself alone on the porch, a rifle across his arms. And he was looking at me.

"What are you up to, missy?"

"I figured you were going to need some help. Did you have to shoot Joaquín? Is he bleeding?"

"Not a drop. He come peaceful as a lamb."

"I don't believe it," I said.

"He was a-reading a newspaper. When he lowered it, there was my army Colt in his face. It took the fight right out of him. I think he rather admired my skill."

"What about the boy?"

"He lit out."

"I want to see Joaquín," I said.

"Get his horse. I'll bring him out."

When I returned, the sheriff was walking Joaquín through the door. He had tied the bandit's arms to his side with so many turns of rope that Joaquín looked as if he were inside a cocoon.

"Sir," I said. "*Señor* . . ."

Joaquín refused to look at me. The sheriff had to help him into the saddle. I hurried around the horse to reach Joaquín's other side. Maybe he scorned me, but he knew exactly where I was. He gave the horse a sudden jab of spurs. The horse kicked at me, knocking me down.

I got right up. I was sobbing.

"*Señor* Murieta, I am so sorry! The newspaper said you killed my brother, Lank. Of course I turned you in. I was after revenge, the same as you. I hated you the way you hate Mr. Calico."

You'd think he wasn't hearing a word I was saying. "Let's go, Sheriff."

"In Bedbug I discovered that my brother is still alive! You didn't kill him on the Mariposa road. The newspaper got the facts wrong! I can't expect you to forgive me. But please, please, sir, understand!"

I could see that Joaquín, now bare-headed, was simmering with rage. I had not proved to be a Yankee friend. I had proved to be a Yankee enemy.

His dark eyes remained fixed on the road ahead. A buggy, raising dust, came racing toward us.

Said Sheriff Elwood Flint, "Don't be too hard on the girl, Joaquín. She saved your mangy neck from the lynch mob. You saw that, didn't you? I couldn't have held them off much longer."

The sheriff mounted his horse beside his prisoner and took the halter of Joaquín's silken black horse.

They had hardly taken a step when the buggy pulled up. I heard the sheriff give a shout. "O. O. Mary! I'll arrest you on that old warrant! Soon as I've got time!"

O. O. Mary? I twisted my head and there she was, driving the buggy! The sight of her in her old feathered hat was a terrible shock and interrupted my sobbing. Beside her, now rising from the seat with a rifle taking aim in his hands, was a thick-necked man with hair

red as a bonfire. That was the way Joaquín had described Billy Calico!

"Joaquín," he shouted, "I won't be hunted any longer!"

He fired the rifle. I saw Joaquín flinch. The sheriff pulled up his Colt army pistol and shot Billy Calico dead.

"Meddling fool!" exclaimed Joaquín, turning a sizzling gaze on the sheriff. "You have cheated me of my revenge!"

"Thank you kindly for your words of gratitude," said the sheriff. "I see you're hit."

O. O. Mary lifted her buggy whip and burst out of there before the sheriff could find time to arrest her. But she did throw me a look as prickly as cactus. She must have seen me in Bedbug and hoped I'd lead them to Joaquín. It made me feel miserable that I had done exactly that.

I saw that Joaquín's coat at the shoulder was torn open and looked as if a small bird nest had sprung up. It was turning red.

"*Es destino.* It's nothing," said Joaquín. "Death takes little bites out of me, eh? What does it matter whether the law hangs me with a small wound or not?"

"It matters to me," I said. I ripped off a piece of my gingham dress and climbed up on the rump of his horse and tried to dab at the wound.

He flinched. "You're making it worse, Yankee!"

"Hold still," I said firmly. "Sheriff, I can't get at this wound with all these ropes in the way."

The sheriff coughed out a little laugh. "You ain't getting me to untie him so he can get away, missy."

CHAPTER 17

GOOD-BYE, JOAQUÍN

When I looked up, I thought it must be the miners who'd come to their senses and turned back from the stampede to Poverty Creek. But I saw Three-Fingered Jack and Pio Pio and other bandits. They all were pointing weapons.

The sheriff paused to count all the guns. "Five pistols and four rifles," he said.

"Not counting knives, sheriff," said Three-Fingered Jack in his gravelly voice.

"I'd say I was outnumbered," remarked the sheriff calmly. "You may have the prisoner."

"You are a man of wisdom," said Three-Fingered Jack.

"He has a flesh wound."

"We take care of it, Sheriff," said Three-Fingered Jack, with his big eyes smiling.

Pio Pio jumped down to lead Joaquín's horse to the outlaw side of the road. His eyes avoided me.

"I'd like my rope back," said the sheriff. "It's the only one I got."

"Certainly, *señor,*" said Three-Fingered Jack. Drawing his knife, he reached over and cut Joaquín free.

"Sheriff," said Joaquín after a moment, "I never forget a kindness. I tell you that to be in your custody is a pleasure and a puzzle. Why, *señor*, did you fire at the Yankee? He was only attacking an unarmed Mexican, eh?"

"He needed to be taught better manners," answered Sheriff Iron Eyes Flint.

I saw Joaquín exchange a few words with Pio Pio, and then the outlaws turned and spurred their horses. But not before Joaquín turned to flash me a look. He smiled and raised a couple of fingers in the air. It was a kind of silent good-bye. He had forgiven me.

I burst into a smile that I think could have lit up the dark. I waved, and my eyes got all moist. I never saw him alive again.

But I did see Pio Pio. He remained behind.

"Joaquín said to look after you," he announced unhappily.

"I can look after myself," I said. "But the gold in that jar on the step belongs to him. Remember? He gave it to me to buy a new dress. You can take it back."

He collected the jar, I found the leather pouch, and he poured the gold back inside. I knew he must hate the sight of me for betraying Joaquín, so I explained how it happened and how awful I felt about it. Finally he gave a little nod.

"Joaquín only shot into the air during the holdup on the Mariposa road," he said. "It was Three-Fingered Jack who killed the gambler."

I walked up the street to the chowchow shop where I'd left the spotted horse tied to the hitch rail. I decided I wanted to keep him after all.

"It's bad luck for a horse not to have a name," Pio Pio said.

"I think I'll call him Destino."

"That's no name for a horse."

"It is now."

Pio Pio insisted on riding into Bedbug with me. Then he said I should buy a new dress, just as Joaquín had expected me to do.

And the truth was, my gingham needed a good washing and some repairs where I'd torn a piece off. So I asked Pio Pio to pick out a calico dress for me, for I hesitated to walk into the general store, big as life. "And a straw hat, too," I added.

I changed clothes behind some tall weeds and came out looking brand-new and different. I passed the barbershop, and nobody ran out to hang me.

There was nothing to do now but wait for my brother to turn up in Bedbug, as promised. I spent a couple of hours talking about the celebrated bandit to Mr. Yellow Bird Ridge. He took pages of notes while Pio Pio gazed around at the big, mysterious printing press and the inks and wooden trays of lead type. He seemed to like the smell of it all.

Someone must have got word to the Rangers, for just before dark the posse came rattling into town to pick up Joaquín's trail. I stationed myself out front and searched the faces for my brother. I made out the leader, Captain Harry Love, a wild-haired man with narrow, puffed, but determined eyes.

He held up his glove and shouted an order to stop. "Rangers, look after your horses. We'll pick up the trail at first light."

Suddenly there was my brother, Lankly Lafayette Smith, turned all grown up. Didn't he look proud of himself riding with those Rangers! I waved my arms like a windmill, and he saw me, but he needed to walk his horse to the water trough. Finally he turned and threw his arms around me and swung me around.

"Hello, little sister."

"Lank," I said, "you're looking prouder'n a white goose."

"Your ankle has healed?"

"Hardly any thanks to O. O. Mary."

We were reunited at last! But the happy glow of seeing him again lasted only those first moments. "Brother, you mustn't ride off with those Rangers," I said.

"What thundering nonsense are you talking?"

"You mustn't!"

"Of course I must. I joined up, didn't I?"

"Unjoin."

"Have you gone scrambly-witted, Annyrose?"

"Please!"

"I've got a job of work to do, sis. Joaquín Murieta is only a few hours ahead of us. Don't you know he's the devil himself in long woolen underwear? I intend to go along. We'll catch him!"

Pio Pio was standing on the boardwalk, hanging back in the darkening shadows. He was eyeing us, listening.

"Lank," I said, and pulled him away from the water trough and the nearby men. "Dear brother, it was Joaquín who saved me from that dreadful O. O. Mary. He has looked out for me. You'd think I was his daughter."

"What? That bloodthirsty outlaw?"

"He's my friend."

Lank held me at arm's length and stared into my face. "Your what?"

"I'm as surprised as you. I know he'll hang someday, Lank. But not at your hands. Please!"

Lank stiffened up his back. "I must do what's expected of me, Annyrose."

"Don't go, brother. I'm pleading with you."

"Do you have a place to stay? Perhaps the hotel can put you up until I get back."

Why wouldn't he listen to me? My eyes began to go wet. Pio Pio was staring at me. I gave him a hopeless look and then a second look, as if to say if someone stole Lank's horse, how could he ride off with the Rangers?

"My friend will look after your horse," I said to Lank.

"What friend?"

"There. My friend Pio Pio."

And Lank said, "Would you give the horse a good

brushing, please? Can you find him a handful of oats or corn?"

Pio Pio nodded, and Lank led me away.

The hotel was an old adobe with worm-eaten ceiling beams. It was quiet in there, and Lank stretched out his long legs on the bed while he had the time.

"The newspaper said you were dead," I muttered. "Don't give me a scare like that again, Lank."

"The news amazed me as well, Annyrose. The dead man was that scoundrel who picked my pocket in San Diego, remember? He still had all my papers, and the blamed, no-souled rascal chose to use my name in his crooked ways instead of his own."

I told him about O. O. Mary and how dreadfully wicked she had been to me, and that infuriated him. When I explained how Joaquín had let me ride along and how he had taken care of me, Lank did look troubled. But he wouldn't go back on his word to Captain Love and the Rangers.

He fell off to sleep early, having ridden all day, and when he awoke at first light, the Rangers were forming in the street. Lank jumped up, buckled on his gun belt, and dashed outside.

That's when he discovered that his horse had been stolen.

CHAPTER 18

ES DESTINO

A few days later, tied up in front of the hotel, there stood Lank's horse—well fed, brushed, and shiny as silk. I looked around for a glimpse of Pio Pio, but this was his good-bye. He figured Lank and I could look after ourselves now. I never saw him again.

And not O. O. Mary, either. Sheriff Iron Eyes Flint got around to chasing her down. She was now in the Bedbug jail, but I didn't bother to pay her a social call.

There was no way Lank could catch up to the Rangers after their long head start. He wrote out his resignation.

All the bad luck that had been lurking in wait for us since we left Louisiana went swinging around like a weather vane in a new wind. A couple of miners who had run over to Poverty Creek where I said there was gold found a lump the size of a baby chick. There's luck for you! The men were as good as their word and shared it out with me.

Lank said he'd like to settle in Jackson, where he saw someone pay two hundred dollars for a wheelbarrow. He thought he might make wheelbarrows for a while. Lank was always good with his hands.

"I'd like Jackson fine," I said. "There are a couple of miners up that way who play the violin, and they need a third. I could earn some gold dust and practice at the same time."

I went in to say good-bye to Mr. Yellow Bird Ridge and found him in a frenzy of typesetting.

"You haven't heard?" he asked.

I had a dreadful hunch and didn't really want to hear it. "Joaquín? Joaquín Murieta?"

He nodded, clacking wooden type onto a marble slab. "Captain Love and the Rangers caught up with him down at Cantua Creek. It was a big shoot-out."

"Is he still alive?"

"No."

"That's not true!" I shouted. Joaquín was a man of a thousand lives. Why not one more?

"It's true," said Mr. Yellow Bird Ridge, very softly,

seeing how upset I was. Finally I calmed myself down, and he said, "The outlaw was only twenty-two years old."

"The others?"

"Shot down, the lot of them."

"Not Pio Pio?" I asked.

"Who?"

"He was hardly more than a boy."

"No, there were no boys among the dead."

"Did Three-Fingered Jack get away?"

"No, miss. They cut off his hand to bring back as proof."

I turned away in disgust.

Then the newspaperman said, "And they cut off Joaquín's head."

I walked out, crying.

It was some weeks before I felt like finding the two brothers and playing an air on the violin. They had just been down to Stockton and said they'd seen new posters all over town. The head of Joaquín preserved in alcohol was to be exhibited.

"You want to go?" asked Lank in amazement. "You'll faint away."

"Most likely," I said. "But I can hardly believe it.

Joaquín always reckoned it was his fate to hang from the limb of an oak tree. I want to see him a last time. I never got a chance to say good-bye."

So we saddled our horses and wound our way down out of the hills. We saw posters nailed up long before we reached Stockton.

WILL BE EXHIBITED
FOR ONE DAY ONLY!

**AT THE
STOCKTON
HOUSE**

THE HEAD
OF THE RENOWNED BANDIT
JOAQUÍN!

THIS DAY, AUGUST 12,
FROM 9 A.M. UNTIL 6 P.M.

AND

**THE HAND OF
THREE-FINGERED
JACK!**

THE NOTORIOUS ROBBER
AND MURDERER

We found our way to the Stockton House, and my stomach began to feel fluttery. Even to be hanged from a tree would be a more dignified end for a proud outlaw like Joaquín. It seemed so savage to put a head on display that I thought hardly a soul would pay money to see such an object.

But I was wrong. We had to wait in line and to pay one dollar each to view the grisly sights. The head and the hand sat well lit in glass jars on a velvet-topped table. I wouldn't look at the hand of Three-Fingered Jack.

It was all I could do to force myself to view the head in the big jar beside it. I could see hair floating like seaweed around the face. I'd thank Joaquín for being kind to me, and I'd say a quick and final good-bye. Then I'd faint away if I had to. But when I felt my breath catch, it was not from the horror of the sight. I looked at the closed eyes and the narrow face.

"Lank!" I shouted out, so that others around us twisted their heads. I pulled at his sleeve to draw him away and lowered my voice. "Lank, *that's not Joaquín Murieta*!"

"Annyrose—"

"*Es destino*, Lank."

"What are you talking about?"

"He got away."

We hurried out. I knew the face in the jar. It belonged to the *chileno*, the impostor.

I paused for a deep breath, taking in the fresh, fresh air. Somewhere in the California hills, I thought, there stood a patient oak tree still waiting for Joaquín.

AUTHOR'S NOTE

Is this entirely a work of the imagination? No. Dashing about on his silken black horse and breathing fire, Joaquín Murieta lived. He was an avenging terror of the roads during the California gold rush and kept getting his name in the newspapers of the 1850s.

Shortly after Murieta's capture, a small-town newspaperman (who signed himself Yellow Bird) published a life of the outlaw. Fact turned into flamboyant legend.

But how much of the legend is myth and fantasy? A great deal, no doubt. The Nobel Prize-winning Chilean poet Pablo Neruda wrote a play about the bandit, portraying Murieta and Three-

Fingered Jack as patriotic Chileans. An earlier playwright made them out to be Spaniards. A folk song has the outlaw born in Hermosillo, Mexico. That, I'm convinced, is closest to the truth.

The gold rush attracted adventurers from every corner of the world, men both honorable and less than. They found Mexicans already working the gold streams. California, after all, had been part of northern Mexico until a few years before. The lust for riches released a firestorm of bigotry aimed not only at Mexicans but at Indians and Chinese as well. In an attempt to rid the diggings of darker skins, a law was passed imposing a heavy monthly tax on "foreign" miners. Law-and-order committees attempted to banish Mexicans from their towns. It's also true that honorable men prevailed and that the laws of bigotry were repealed. But not before a great deal of harm was done and the legend of Joaquín Murieta was born.

I have written a novel with the legendary bandit at its center, but I have not attempted the impossible: a biography. The facts of his life are too sketchy and fogged in dispute and the unknown. There are at least four other California bandits whose first name was Joaquín. There is not even scholarly agreement regarding the outlaw's wife. Was she Rosita? Carmela? Clarina? And there is total confusion about the spelling of Joaquín's last name. Was it Murietta, Murrieta, or Muriatta? I doubt that Joaquín cared very much, but it was almost certainly Murieta.

The poster advertising the head of Joaquín says the final battle took place in "Arroya Cantina," or Cantina Creek. Really? Yellow Bird gives it the fanciful and un-Spanish spelling of "Cantoova." The source I regard as most reliable identifies the place as Cantua Creek.

Like a stage manager, I have shifted the scenery about to suit my dramatic purposes. I felt free to imagine dialogues and adventures in the spirit of Joaquín if not in actual fact. If these scenes didn't actually happen, they should have.

It certainly happened that his severed head and the hand of Three-Fingered Jack were widely exhibited in 1853.

But was it actually the head of Joaquín Murieta displayed in the glass jar? Many who claimed to know the desperado took one look and scornfully declared no. At any rate, the Robin Hood of the Mountains vanished from California.

As for the town called Bedbug, you won't find it on a map. But it did exist. Once the citizens began combing their hair and wearing ties, they changed the name to Ione.